W9-ATN-798

GEORGE ELIOT

(1819-1880) was born Marian Evans, the third child of Christina and Robert Evans. Her father was agent to a large landholder in Warwickshire. She attended private schools until her mother's death in 1836, thereafter continuing her education at home. Strongly influenced by the Evangelical movement, her first publication was a religious poem, appearing under her own initials in *The Christian Observer* in 1840. She and her father moved to Coventry in 1841, where she became acquainted with the free-thinkers, the Brays and the Hennels, and her resulting religious doubts led to a rift with her father. From 1843 to 1846 George Eliot worked on a translation of Strauss' *Life of Jesus* and then a translation of Spinoza's *Tractatus theologico-politicus*. After her father's death in 1849 she travelled to the Continent. She began contributing to *The Westminster Review* in 1850 and in 1851 moved to London, acting as Assistant Editor of *The Review* until 1854, when her translation of Feuerbach's *Essence of Christianity* was published. That year she began living with George Henry Lewes and their relationship continued until his death in 1878. As Lewes was already married their union was never legalised.

George Eliot began writing fiction in 1856, with Lewes' encouragement. He sent the first of the stories in *Scenes from Clerical Life* to *Blackwood's* in 1857. Critical acclaim was followed by popular success with the publication of George Eliot's other works of fiction: *Adam Bede* (1859), *The Mill on the Floss* (1860), *Silas Marner* (1861), *Romola* (1863), *Felix Holt the Radical* (1866), *The Lifted Veil* and *Brother Jacob* (1879) (published with *Silas Marner*), *Middlemarch* (1871) and *Daniel Deronda* (1876). She also published poetry: *How Lisa loved the King* (1867), *Spanish Gipsy* (1860), *Armgart* (1870) and *The Legend of Jubal* (1870). Her final work was the satire *Impressions of Theophrastus Such* (1879).

In May 1880 George Eliot married her old friend J. W. Cross. She died in December of the same year.

Give me no light, great Heaven, but such as turns
To energy of human fellowship;
No powers beyond the growing heritage
That makes completer manhood.

GEORGE ELIOT

The Lifted Veil

With a new afterword
by Beryl Gray

PENGUIN BOOKS — VIRAGO PRESS

PENGUIN BOOKS
Published by the Penguin Group
Penguin Books USA Inc.,
375 Hudson Street, New York, New York 10014, U.S.A.
Penguin Books Ltd, 27 Wrights Lane, London W8 5TZ, England
Penguin Books Australia Ltd, Ringwood, Victoria, Australia
Penguin Books Canada Ltd, 10 Alcorn Avenue,
Toronto, Ontario, Canada M4V 3B2
Penguin Books (N.Z.) Ltd, 182–190 Wairau Road, Auckland 10, New Zealand

Penguin Books Ltd, Registered Offices:
Harmondsworth, Middlesex, England

First published in Great Britain with *Silas Marner* and
Brother Jacob in a Cabinet edition 1878
First published as a single volume in Great Britain
by Holerth Press 1924
This edition first published in Great Britain
by Virago Press Ltd 1985
Published in Penguin Books 1985

7 9 10 8 6

Afterword copyright © Beryl Gray, 1985
All rights reserved

ISBN 0 14 016.116 3

Printed in the United States of America

Except in the United States of America, this book is sold
subject to the condition that it shall not, by way of trade
or otherwise, be lent, re-sold, hired out, or otherwise circulated
without the publisher's prior consent in any form of binding or
cover other than that in which it is published and without
a similar condition including this condition being imposed on
the subsequent purchaser.

CHAPTER I

THE time of my end approaches. I have lately been subject to attacks of *angina pectoris*; and in the ordinary course of things, my physician tells me, I may fairly hope that my life will not be protracted many months. Unless, then, I am cursed with an exceptional physical constitution, as I am cursed with an exceptional mental character, I shall not much longer groan under the wearisome burthen of this earthly existence. If it were to be otherwise — if I were to live on to the age most men desire and provide for — I should for once have known whether the miseries of delusive expectation can outweigh the miseries of true prevision. For I foresee when I shall die, and everything that will happen in my last moments.

Just a month from this day, on the 20th of September 1850, I shall be sitting in this chair, in this study, at ten o'clock at night, longing to die, weary of incessant insight and foresight, without delusions and without hope. Just as I am watching a tongue of blue flame rising in the fire, and my lamp is burning low, the horrible contraction will begin at my chest. I shall only have time to reach the bell, and pull it violently, before the sense of suffocation will come. No one will answer my bell. I know why. My two servants are lovers, and will have quarrelled. My house-keeper will have rushed out of the house in a fury, two hours before, hoping that Perry will believe she has gone to drown herself. Perry is alarmed at last, and is gone out after her. The little scullery-maid is asleep on a bench: she never answers the bell; it does not wake her. The sense of suffocation increases: my lamp goes out with a horrible stench: I make a great effort, and snatch at the bell again. I long for life, and there is no help. I thirsted for the unknown: the thirst is gone. O God, let me stay with the known, and be weary of it: I am content. Agony of pain and suffocation — and all the while the earth, the fields, the pebbly brook at the bottom of the rookery, the fresh scent after the rain, the light of the morning through my chamber-window, the warmth of the hearth after the frosty air — will darkness close over them for ever?

Darkness — darkness — no pain — nothing but dark-ness: but I am passing on and on through the darkness: my thought stays in the darkness, but always with a sense of moving onward. . . .

Before that time comes, I wish to use my last hours of ease and strength in telling the strange story of my experience. I have never fully unbosomed myself to any human being; I have never been encouraged to trust much in the sympathy of my fellow-men. But we have all a chance of meeting with some pity, some tenderness, some charity, when we are dead: it is the living only who cannot be forgiven — the living only from whom men's indulgence and reverence are held off, like the rain by the hard east wind. While the heart beats, bruise it — it is your only opportunity; while the eye can still turn towards you with moist timid entreaty, freeze it with an icy unanswering gaze; ;while the ear, that delicate messenger to the inmost sanctuary of the soul, can still take in the tones of kindness, put it off with hard civility, or sneering compliment, or envious affectation of indifference; while the creative brain can still throb with the sense of injustice, with the yearning for brotherly recognition — make haste — oppress it with your ill-considered judgments, your trivial comparisons, your careless misrepresentations. The heart will by-and-by be still — *ubi saeva indignatio ulterius cor lacerare nequit*;[1] the eye will cease to entreat; the ear will be deaf; the brain will have ceased from all wants as well as from all work. Then your charitable speeches may find vent; then you may remember and pity the toil and the struggle and the failure; then you may give due honour to the work achieved; then you may find extenuation for errors, and may consent to bury them.

That is a trivial schoolboy text; why do I dwell on it? It has little reference to me, for I shall leave no works

---

1. Inscription on Swift's tombstone.

behind me for men to honour. I have no near relatives who will make up, by weeping over my grave, for the wounds they inflicted on me when I was among them. It is only the story of my life that will perhaps win a little more sympathy from strangers when I am dead, than I ever believed it would obtain from my friends while I was living.

My childhood perhaps seems happier to me than it really was, by contrast with all the after-years. For then the curtain of the future was as impenetrable to me as to other children: I had all their delight in the present hour, their sweet indefinite hopes for the morrow; and I had a tender mother: even now, after the dreary lapse of long years, a slight trace of sensation accompanies the remembrance of her caress as she held me on her knee — her arms round my little body, her cheek pressed on mine. I had a complaint of the eyes that made me blind for a little while, and she kept me on her knee from morning till night. That unequalled love soon vanished out of my life, and even to my childish consciousness it was as if that life had become more chill. I rode my little white pony with the groom by my side as before, but there were no loving eyes looking at me as I mounted, no glad arms opened to me when I came back. Perhaps I missed my mother's love more than most children of seven or eight would have done, to whom the other pleasures of life remained as before; for I was certainly a very sensitive child. I remember still the mingled trepidation and delicious excitement with which I was affected by the tramping of the horses on the pavement in the echoing stables, by the loud resonance of the grooms' voices, by the booming bark of the dogs as my father's carriage thundered under the archway of the courtyard, by the din of the gong as it gave notice of luncheon and dinner. The measured tramp of soldiery which I sometimes heard — for my father's house lay near a county town where there were large barracks — made me sob and tremble; and yet when they were gone past, I longed for them to come back again.

I fancy my father thought me an odd child, and had little fondness for me; though he was very careful in fulfilling what he regarded as a parent's duties. But he was already past the middle of life, and I was not his only son. My mother had been his second wife, and he was five-and-forty when he married her. He was a firm, unbending, intensely orderly man, in root and stem a banker, but with a flourishing graft of the active land-holder, aspiring to county influence: one of those people who are always like themselves from day to day, who are uninfluenced by the weather, and neither know melancholy nor high spirits. I held him in great awe, and appeared more timid and sensitive in his presence than at other times; a circumstance which, perhaps, helped to confirm him in the intention to educate me on a different plan from the prescriptive one with which he had complied in the case of my elder brother, already a tall

youth at Eton. My brother was to be his representative
and successor; he must go to Eton and Oxford, for the
sake of making connections, of course: my father was not
a man to underrate the bearing of Latin satirists or Greek
dramatists on the attainment of an aristocratic position.
But, intrinsically, he had slight esteem for "those dead but
sceptred spirits"; having qualified himself for forming an
independent opinion by reading Potter's 'Aeschylus', and
dipping into Francis's 'Horace'. To this negative view he
added a positive one, derived from a recent connection
with mining speculations; namely, that a scientific
education was the really useful training for a younger son.
Moreover, it was clear that a shy, sensitive boy like me
was not fit to encounter the rough experience of a public
school. Mr Letherall had said so very decidedly.
Mr Letherall was a large man in spectacles, who one day
took my small head between his large hands, and pressed
it here and there in an exploratory, suspicious manner
— then placed each of his great thumbs on my temples,
and pushed me a little way from him, and stared at me
with glittering spectacles. The contemplation appeared to
displease him, for he frowned sternly, and said to my
father, drawing his thumbs across my eyebrows —

"The deficiency is there, sir — there; and here," he
added, touching the upper sides of my head, "here is the
excess. That must be brought out, sir, and this must be
laid to sleep."

I was in a state of tremor, partly at the vague idea that

I was the object of reprobation, partly in the agitation of my first hatred — hatred of this big, spectacled man, who pulled my head about as if he wanted to buy and cheapen it.

I am not aware how much Mr Letherall had to do with the system afterwards adopted towards me, but it was presently clear that private tutors, natural history, science, and the modern languages, were the appliances by which the defects of my organisation were to be remedied. I was very stupid about machines, so I was to be greatly occupied with them; I had no memory for classification, so it was particularly necessary that I should study systematic zoology and botany; I was hungry for human deeds and human emotions, so I was to be plentifully crammed with the mechanical powers, the elementary bodies, and the phenomena of electricity and magnetism. A better-constituted boy would certainly have profited under my intelligent tutors, with their scientific apparatus; and would, doubtless, have found the phenomena of electricity and magnetism as fascinating as I was, every Thursday, assured they were. As it was, I could have paired off, for ignorance of whatever was taught me, with the worst Latin scholar that was ever turned out of a classical academy. I read Plutarch, and Shakespere, and Don Quixote by the sly, and supplied myself in that way with wandering thoughts, while my tutor was assuring me that "an improved man, as distinguished from an ignorant one, was a man who knew the reason why water ran down-hill." I had no desire to be this improved man; I was glad of the running water; I could watch it and listen to it gurgling among the pebbles, and bathing the bright green water-plants, by the hour together. I did not want to know *why* it ran; I had perfect confidence that there were good reasons for what was so very beautiful.

There is no need to dwell on this part of my life. I have said enough to indicate that my nature was of the sensitive, unpractical order, and that it grew up in an uncongenial medium, which could never foster it into happy, healthy development. When I was sixteen I was sent to Geneva to complete my course of education; and the change was a very happy one to me, for the sight of the Alps, with the setting sun on them, as we descended the Jura, seemed to me like an entrance into heaven; and the three years of my life there were spent in a perpetual sense of exaltation, as if from a draught of delicious wine, at the presence of Nature in all her awful loveliness. You will think, perhaps, that I must have been a poet, from this early sensibility to Nature. But my lot was not so happy as that. A poet pours forth his song and *believes* in the listening ear and answering soul, to which his song will be floated sooner or later. But the poet's sensibility without his voice — the poet's sensibility that finds no vent but in silent tears on the sunny bank, when the noonday light sparkles on the water, or in an inward shudder at the sound of harsh human tones, the sight of a cold human eye—this dumb passion brings with it a fatal solitude of soul in the society of one's fellow-men. My least solitary moments were those in which I pushed off in my boat, at evening, towards the centre of the lake; it seemed to me that the sky, and the glowing mountain-tops, and the wide blue water, surrounded me with a cherishing love such as no human face had shed on me since my mother's love had vanished out of my life. I used to do as Jean Jacques did—lie down in my boat and let it glide where it would, while I looked up at the departing glow leaving one mountain-top after the other, as if the prophet's chariot of fire were passing over them on its way to the home of light. Then, when the white summits were all sad and corpse-like, I had to push homeward, for I was under careful surveillance, and was allowed no late wanderings. This disposition of mine was not favourable to the formation of intimate friendships among the numerous youths of my own age who are always to be found studying at Geneva. Yet I made *one* such friendship; and, singularly enough, it was with a youth whose intellectual tendencies were the very reverse of my own. I shall call him Charles Meunier; his real surname—an English one, for he was of English extraction—having since become celebrated. He was an orphan, who lived on a miserable pittance while he pursued the medical studies for which he had a special genius. Strange! that with my vague mind, susceptible and unobservant, hating inquiry and given up to contemplation, I should have been drawn towards a youth whose strongest passion was science. But the bond was not an intellectual one; it came from a source that can happily blend the stupid with the brilliant, the dreamy with the practical: it came from community of feeling. Charles was poor and ugly, derided by Genevese *gamins*, and not acceptable in drawing-rooms. I saw that he was isolated, as I was, though from a different cause, and, stimulated by a sympathetic resentment, I made timid advances towards him. It is enough to say that there sprang up as much comradeship between us as our different habits would allow; and in Charles's rare holidays we went up the Salève together, or took the boat to Vevay, while I listened dreamily to the monologues in which he unfolded his bold conceptions of future experiment and discovery. I mingled them confusedly in my thought with glimpses of blue water and delicate floating cloud, with the notes of birds and the distant glitter of the glacier. He knew quite well that my mind was half absent, yet he liked to talk to me in this way; for don't we talk of our hopes and our projects even to dogs and birds, when they love us? I have mentioned this one friendship because of its connection with a strange and terrible scene which I shall have to narrate in my subsequent life.

This happier life at Geneva was put an end to by a severe illness, which is partly a blank to me, partly a time of dimly-remembered suffering, with the presence of my father by my bed from time to time. Then came the languid monotony of convalescence, the days gradually breaking into variety and distinctness as my strength enabled me to take longer and longer drives. On one of these more vividly remembered days, my father said to me, as he sat beside my sofa —

"When you are quite well enough to travel, Latimer, I shall take you home with me. The journey will amuse you and do you good, for I shall go through the Tyrol and Austria, and you will see many new places. Our neighbours, the Filmores, are come; Alfred will join us at Basle, and we shall all go together to Vienna, and back by Prague" . . .

My father was called away before he had finished his sentence, and he left my mind resting on the word *Prague*, with a strange sense that a new and wondrous scene was breaking upon me: a city under the broad sunshine, that seemed to me as if it were the summer sunshine of a long-past century arrested in its course — unrefreshed for ages by the dews of night, or the rushing rain-cloud; scorching the dusty, weary, time-eaten grandeur of a people doomed to live on in the stale repetition of memories, like deposed and superannuated kings in their regal gold-inwoven tatters. The city looked so thirsty that the broad river seemed to me a sheet of metal; and the blackened statues, as I passed under their blank gaze, along the unending bridge, with their ancient garments and their saintly crowns, seemed to me the real inhabitants and owners of this place, while the busy, trivial men and women, hurrying to and fro, were a swarm of ephemeral visitants infesting it for a day. It is such grim, stony beings as these, I thought, who are the fathers of ancient faded children, in those tanned time-fretted dwellings that crowd the steep before me; who pay their court in the worn and crumbling pomp of the palace which stretches its monotonous length on the height; who worship wearily in the stifling air of the churches, urged by no fear or hope, but compelled by their doom to be ever old and undying, to live on in the rigidity of habit, as they live on in perpetual mid-day, without the repose of night or the new birth of morning.

A stunning clang of metal suddenly thrilled through me, and I became conscious of the objects in my room again: one of the fire-irons had fallen as Pierre opened the door to bring me my draught. My heart was palpitating violently, and I begged Pierre to leave my draught beside me; I would take it presently.

As soon as I was alone again, I began to ask myself whether I had been sleeping. Was this a dream — this wonderfully distinct vision — minute in its distinctness down to a patch of rainbow light on the pavement, transmitted through a coloured lamp in the shape of a star — of a strange city, quite unfamiliar to my imagination? I had seen no picture of Prague: it lay in my mind as a mere name, with vaguely-remembered historical associations — ill-defined memories of imperial grandeur and religious wars.

Nothing of this sort had ever occurred in my dreaming experience before, for I had often been humiliated because my dreams were only saved from being utterly disjointed and commonplace by the frequent terrors of nightmare. But I could not believe that I had been asleep, for I remembered distinctly the gradual breaking-in of the vision upon me, like the new images in a dissolving view, or the growing distinctness of the landscape as the sun lifts up the veil of the morning mist. And while I was conscious of this incipient vision, I was also conscious that Pierre came to tell my father Mr Filmore was waiting for him, and that my father hurried out of the room. No, it was not a dream; was it — the thought was full of tremulous exultation — was it the poet's nature in me, hitherto only a troubled yearning sensibility, now manifesting itself suddenly as spontaneous creation? Surely it was in this way that Homer saw the plain of Troy, that Dante saw the abodes of the departed, that Milton saw the earthward flight of the Tempter. Was it that my illness had wrought some happy change in my organisation — given a firmer tension to my nerves — carried off some dull obstruction? I had often read of such effects — in works of fiction at least. Nay; in genuine biographies I had read of the subtilising or exalting influence of some diseases on the mental powers. Did not Novalis feel his inspiration intensified under the progress of consumption?

When my mind had dwelt for some time on this blissful idea, it seemed to me that I might perhaps test it by an exertion of my will. The vision had begun when my father was speaking of our going to Prague. I did not for a moment believe it was really a representation of that city; I believed — I hoped it was a picture that my newly-liberated genius had painted in fiery haste, with the colours snatched from lazy memory. Suppose I were to fix my mind on some other place — Venice, for example, which was far more familiar to my imagination than Prague: perhaps the same sort of result would follow. I concentrated my thoughts on Venice; I stimulated my imagination with poetic memories, and strove to feel myself present in Venice, as I had felt myself present in Prague. But in vain. I was only colouring the Canaletto engravings that hung in my old bedroom at home; the picture was a shifting one, my mind wandering uncertainly in search of more vivid images; I could see no accident of form or shadow without conscious labour after the necessary conditions. It was all prosaic effort, not rapt passivity, such as I had experienced half an hour before. I was discouraged; but I remembered that inspiration was fitful.

For several days I was in a state of excited expectation, watching for a recurrence of my new gift. I sent my thoughts ranging over my world of knowledge, in the hope that they would find some object which would send a reawakening vibration through my slumbering genius. But no; my world remained as dim as ever, and that flash of strange light refused to come again, though

I watched for it with palpitating eagerness.

My father accompanied me every day in a drive, and a gradually lengthening walk as my powers of walking increased; and one evening he had agreed to come and fetch me at twelve the next day, that we might go together to select a musical box, and other purchases rigorously demanded of a rich Englishman visiting Geneva. He was one of the most punctual of men and bankers, and I was always nervously anxious to be quite ready for him at the appointed time. But, to my surprise, at a quarter past twelve he had not appeared. I felt all the impatience of a convalescent who has nothing particular to do, and who has just taken a tonic in the prospect of immediate exercise that would carry off the stimulus.

Unable to sit still and reserve my strength, I walked up and down the room, looking out on the current of the Rhone, just where it leaves the dark-blue lake; but thinking all the while of the possible causes that could detain my father.

Suddenly I was conscious that my father was in the room, but not alone: there were two persons with him. Strange! I had heard no footstep, I had not seen the door open; but I saw my father, and at his right hand our neighbour Mrs Filmore, whom I remembered very well, though I had not seen her for five years. She was a commonplace middle-aged woman, in silk and cashmere; but the lady on the left of my father was no more than twenty, a tall, slim, willowy figure, with luxuriant blond

15

hair, arranged in cunning braids and folds that looked almost too massive for the slight figure and the small-featured, thin-lipped face they crowned. But the face had not a girlish expression: the features were sharp, the pale grey eyes at once acute, restless, and sarcastic. They were fixed on me in half-smiling curiosity, and I felt a painful sensation as if a sharp wind were cutting me. The pale-green dress, and the green leaves that seemed to form a border about her pale blond hair, made me think of a Water-Nixie, — for my mind was full of German lyrics, and this pale, fatal-eyed woman, with the green weeds, looked like a birth from some cold sedgy-stream, the daughter of an aged river.

"Well, Latimer, you thought me long," my father said. . . .

But while the last word was in my ears, the whole group vanished, and there was nothing between me and the Chinese painted folding-screen that stood before the door. I was cold and trembling; I could only totter forward and throw myself on the sofa. This strange new power had manifested itself again. . . . But *was* it a power? Might it not rather be a disease — a sort of intermittent delirium, concentrating my energy of brain into moments of unhealthy activity, and leaving my saner hours all the more barren? I felt a dizzy sense of unreality in what my eye rested on; I grasped the bell convulsively, like one trying to free himself from nightmare, and rang it twice. Pierre came with a look of alarm in his face.

"Monsieur ne se trouve pas bien?" he said, anxiously.

"I'm tired of waiting, Pierre," I said, as distinctly and emphatically as I could, like a man determined to be sober in spite of wine; "I'm afraid something has happened to my father—he's usually so punctual. Run to the Hôtel des Bergues and see if he is there."

Pierre left the room at once, with a soothing "Bien, Monsieur"; and I felt the better for this scene of simple, waking prose. Seeking to calm myself still further, I went into my bedroom, adjoining the *salon*, and opened a case of eau-de-Cologne; took out a bottle; went through the process of taking out the cork very neatly, and then rubbed the reviving spirit over my hands and forehead, and under my nostrils, drawing a new delight from the scent because I had procured it by slow details of labour, and by no strange sudden madness. Already I had begun to taste something of the horror that belongs to the lot of a human being whose nature is not adjusted to simple human conditions.

Still enjoying the scent, I returned to the *salon*, but it was not unoccupied, as it had been before I left it. In front of the Chinese folding-screen there was my father, with Mrs Filmore on his right hand, and on his left—the slim blond-haired girl, with the keen face and the keen eyes fixed on me in half-smiling curiosity.

"Well, Latimer, you thought me long", my father said. . . .

I heard no more, felt no more, till I became conscious

that I was lying with my head low on the sofa, Pierre and my father by my side. As soon as I was thoroughly revived, my father left the room, and presently returned, saying—

"I've been to tell the ladies how you are, Latimer. They were waiting in the next room. We shall put off our shopping expedition to-day."

Presently he said, "That young lady is Bertha Grant, Mrs Filmore's orphan niece. Filmore has adopted her, and she lives with them, so you will have her for a neighbour when we go home—perhaps for a near relation; for there is a tenderness between her and Alfred, I suspect, and I should be gratified by the match, since Filmore means to provide for her in every way as if she were his daughter. It had not occurred to me that you knew nothing about her living with the Filmores."

He made no further allusion to the fact of my having fainted at the moment of seeing her, and I would not for the world have told him the reason: I shrank from the idea of disclosing to any one what might be regarded as a pitiable peculiarity, most of all from betraying it to my father, who would have suspected my sanity ever after.

I do not mean to dwell with particularity on the details of my experience. I have described these two cases at length, because they had definite, clearly traceable results in my after-lot.

Shortly after this last occurrence—I think the very next day—I began to be aware of a phase in my abnormal sensibility, to which, from the languid and slight nature of my intercourse with others since my illness, I had not been alive before. This was the obtrusion on my mind of the mental process going forward in first one person, and then another, with whom I happened to be in contact: the vagrant, frivolous ideas and emotions of some uninterest-ing acquaintance — Mrs Filmore, for example — would force themselves on my consciousness like an impor-tunate, ill-played musical instrument, or the loud activity of an imprisoned insect. But this unpleasant sensibility was fitful, and left me moments of rest, when the souls of my companions were once more shut out from me, and I felt a relief such as silence brings to wearied nerves. I might have believed this importunate insight to be merely a diseased activity of the imagination, but that my prevision of incalculable words and actions proved it to have a fixed relation to the mental process in other minds. But this superadded consciousness, wearying and annoy-ing enough when it urged on me the trivial experience of indifferent people, became an intense pain and grief when it seemed to be opening to me the souls of those who were in a close relation to me — when the rational talk, the graceful attentions, the wittily-turned phrases, and the kindly deeds, which used to make the web of their characters, were seen as if thrust asunder by a micro-scopic vision, that showed all the intermediate frivolities, all the suppressed egoism, all the struggling chaos of puerilities, meanness, vague capricious memories, and indolent make-shift thoughts, from which human words and deeds emerge like leaflets covering a fermenting heap.

At Basle we were joined by my brother Alfred, now a handsome self-confident man of six-and-twenty — a thorough contrast to my fragile, nervous, ineffectual self. I believe I was held to have a sort of half-womanish, half-ghostly beauty; for the portrait-painters, who are thick as weeds at Geneva, had often asked me to sit to them, and I had been the model of a dying minstrel in a fancy picture. But I thoroughly disliked my own *physique*, and nothing but the belief that it was a condition of poetic genius would have reconciled me to it. That brief hope was quite fled, and I saw in my face now nothing but the stamp of a morbid organisation, framed for passive suffering — too feeble for the sublime resistance of poetic production. Alfred, from whom I had been almost constantly separated, and who, in his present stage of character and appearance, came before me as a perfect stranger, was bent on being extremely friendly and brother-like to me. He had the superficial kindness of a good-humoured, self-satisfied nature, that fears no rivalry, and has encountered no contrarieties. I am not sure that my disposition was good enough for me to have been quite free from envy towards him, even if our desires had not clashed, and if I had been in the healthy human condition which admits of generous confidence and charitable construction. There must always have been an antipathy between our natures. As it was, he became in a few weeks an object of intense hatred to me; and when he entered the room, still more when he spoke, it was as if a sensation of grating metal had set my teeth on edge. My diseased consciousness was more intensely and continually occupied with his thoughts and emotions, than with those of any other person who came in my way. I was perpetually exasperated with the petty promptings of his conceit and his love of patronage, with his self-complacent belief in Bertha Grant's passion for him, with his half-pitying contempt for me—seen not in the ordinary indications of intonations and phrase and slight action, which an acute and suspicious mind is on the watch for, but in all their naked skinless complication.

For we were rivals, and our desires clashed, though he was not aware of it. I have said nothing yet of the effect Bertha Grant produced in me on a nearer acquaintance. That effect was chiefly determined by the fact that she made the only exception, among all the human beings about me, to my unhappy gift of insight. About Bertha I was always in a state of uncertainty: I could watch the expression of her face, and speculate on its meaning; I could ask for her opinion with the real interest of ignorance; I could listen for her words and watch for her smile with hope and fear: she had for me the fascination of an unravelled destiny. I say it was this fact that chiefly determined the strong effect she produced on me: for, in the abstract, no womanly character could seem to have less affinity for that of a shrinking, romantic, passionate

youth than Bertha's. She was keen, sarcastic, unimaginative, prematurely cynical, remaining critical and
unmoved in the most impressive scenes, inclined to
dissect all my favourite poems, and especially contemptuous towards the German lyrics which were my pet
literature at that time. To this moment I am unable to
define my feelings towards her: it was not ordinary boyish
admiration, for she was the very opposite, even to the
colour of her hair, of the ideal woman who still remained
to me the type of loveliness; and she was without that
enthusiasm for the great and good, which, even at the
moment of her strongest dominion over me, I should have
declared to be the highest element of character. But there
is no tyranny more complete than that which a self-
centred negative nature exercises over a morbidly
sensitive nature perpetually craving sympathy and
support. The most independent people feel the effect of
a man's silence in heightening their value for his
opinion — feel an additional triumph in conquering the
reverence of a critic habitually captious and satirical:
no wonder, then, that an enthusiastic self-distrusting
youth should watch and wait before the closed secret of a
sarcastic woman's face, as if it were the shrine of the
doubtfully benignant deity who ruled his destiny. For a
young enthusiast is unable to imagine the total negation
in another mind of the emotions which are stirring his
own: they may be feeble, latent, inactive, he thinks, but
they are there — they may be called forth; sometimes,

in moments of happy hallucination, he believes they may be there in all the greater strength because he sees no outward sign of them. And this effect, as I have intimated, was heightened to its utmost intensity in me, because Bertha was the only being who remained for me in the mysterious seclusion of soul that renders such youthful delusion possible. Doubtless there was another sort of fascination at work — that subtle physical attraction which delights in cheating our psychological predictions, and in compelling the men who paint sylphs, to fall in love with some *bonne et brave femme*, heavy-heeled and freckled.

Bertha's behaviour towards me was such as to encourage all my illusions, to heighten my boyish passion, and make me more and more dependent on her smiles. Looking back with my present wretched knowledge, I conclude that her vanity and love of power were intensely gratified by the belief that I had fainted on first seeing her purely from the strong impression her person had produced on me. The most prosaic woman likes to believe herself the object of a violent, a poetic passion; and without a grain of romance in her, Bertha had that spirit of intrigue which gave piquancy to the idea that the brother of the man she meant to marry was dying with love and jealousy for her sake. That she meant to marry my brother, was what at that time I did not believe; for though he was assiduous in his attentions to her, and I knew well enough that both he and my father had made up their minds to this result, there was not yet an understood engagement — there had been no explicit declaration; and Bertha habitually, while she flirted with my brother, and accepted his homage in a way that implied to him a thorough recognition of its intention, made me believe, by the subtlest looks and phrases — feminine nothings which could never be quoted against her — that he was really the object of her secret ridicule; that she thought him, as I did, a coxcomb, whom she would have pleasure in disappointing. Me she openly petted in my brother's presence, as if I were too young and sickly ever to be thought of as a lover; and that was the view he took of me. But I believe she must inwardly have delighted in the tremors into which she threw me by the coaxing way in which she patted my curls, while she laughed at my quotations. Such caresses were always given in the presence of our friends; for when we were alone together, she affected a much greater distance towards me, and now and then took the opportunity, by words or slight actions, to stimulate my foolish timid hope that she really preferred me. And why should she not follow her inclination? I was not in so advantageous a position as my brother, but I had fortune, I was not a year younger than she was, and she was an heiress, who would soon be of age to decide for herself.

The fluctuations of hope and fear, confined to this one channel, made each day in her presence a delicious torment. There was one deliberate act of hers which especially helped to intoxicate me. When we were at

Vienna her twentieth birthday occurred, and as she was very fond of ornaments, we all took the opportunity of the splendid jewellers' shops in that Teutonic Paris to purchase her a birthday present of jewellery. Mine, naturally, was the least expensive; it was an opal ring — the opal was my favourite stone, because it seems to blush and turn pale as if it had a soul. I told Bertha so when I gave it her, and said that it was an emblem of the poetic nature, changing with the changing light of heaven and of woman's eyes. In the evening she appeared elegantly dressed, and wearing conspicuously all the birthday presents except mine. I looked eagerly at her fingers, but saw no opal. I had no opportunity of noticing this to her during the evening; but the next day, when I found her seated near the window alone, after breakfast, I said, "You scorn to wear my poor opal. I should have remembered that you despised poetic natures, and should have given you coral, or turquoise, or some other opaque unresponsive stone." "Do I despise it?" she answered, taking hold of a delicate gold chain which she always wore round her neck and drawing out the end from her bosom with my ring hanging to it; "it hurts me a little, I can tell you," she said, with her usual dubious smile, "to wear it in that secret place; and since your poetical nature is so stupid as to prefer a more public position, I shall not endure the pain any longer."

She took off the ring from the chain and put it on her finger, smiling still, while the blood rushed to my cheeks, and I could not trust myself to say a word of entreaty that she would keep the ring where it was before.

I was completely fooled by this, and for two days shut myself up in my own room whenever Bertha was absent, that I might intoxicate myself afresh with the thought of this scene and all it implied.

I should mention that during these two months — which seemed a long life to me from the novelty and intensity of the pleasures and pains I underwent — my diseased participation in other people's consciousness continued to torment me; now it was my father, and now my brother, now Mrs Filmore or her husband, and now our German courier, whose stream of thought rushed upon me like a ringing in the ears not to be got rid of, though it allowed my own impulses and ideas to continue their uninterrupted course. It was like a preternaturally heightened sense of hearing, making audible to one a roar of sound where others find perfect stillness. The weariness and disgust of this involuntary intrusion into other souls was counteracted only by my ignorance of Bertha, and my growing passion for her; a passion enormously stimulated, if not produced, by that ignorance. She was my oasis of mystery in the dreary desert of knowledge. I had never allowed my diseased condition to betray itself, or to drive me into any unusual speech or action, except once, when, in a moment of peculiar bitterness against my brother, I had forestalled some words which I knew he was going to utter — a clever observation, which he had prepared beforehand. He had occasionally a slightly-affected hesitation in his speech, and when he paused an instant after the second word, my impatience and jealousy impelled me to continue the speech for him, as if it were something we had both learned by rote. He coloured and looked astonished, as well as annoyed; and the words had no sooner escaped my lips than I felt a shock of alarm lest such an anticipation of words — very far from being words of course, easy to divine — should have betrayed me as an exceptional being, a sort of quiet energumen, whom every one, Bertha above all, would shudder at and avoid. But I magnified, as usual, the impression any word or deed of mine could produce on others; for no one gave any sign of having noticed my interruption as more than a rudeness, to be forgiven me on the score of my feeble nervous condition.

While this superadded consciousness of the actual was almost constant with me, I had never had a recurrence of that distinct prevision which I have described in relation to my first interview with Bertha; and I was waiting with eager curiosity to know whether or not my vision of Prague would prove to have been an instance of the same kind. A few days after the incident of the opal ring, we were paying one of our frequent visits to the Lichtenberg Palace. I could never look at many pictures in succession; for pictures, when they are at all powerful, affect me so strongly that one or two exhaust all my capability of contemplation. This morning I had been looking at

Giorgione's picture of the cruel-eyed woman, said to be a likeness of Lucrezia Borgia. I had stood long alone before it, fascinated by the terrible reality of that cunning, relentless face, till I felt a strange poisoned sensation, as if I had long been inhaling a fatal odour, and was just beginning to be conscious of its effects. Perhaps even then I should not have moved away, if the rest of the party had not returned to this room, and announced that they were going to the Belvedere Gallery to settle a bet which had arisen between my brother and Mr Filmore about a portrait. I followed them dreamily, and was hardly alive to what occurred till they had all gone up to the gallery, leaving me below; for I refused to come within sight of another picture that day. I made my way to the Grand Terrace, since it was agreed that we should saunter in the gardens when the dispute had been decided. I had been sitting here a short space, vaguely conscious of trim gardens, with a city and green hills in the distance, when, wishing to avoid the proximity of the sentinel, I rose and walked down the broad stone steps, intending to seat myself farther on in the gardens. Just as I reached the gravel-walk, I felt an arm slipped within mine, and a light hand gently pressing my wrist. In the same instant a strange intoxicating numbness passed over me, like the continuance or climax of the sensation I was still feeling from the gaze of Lucrezia Borgia. The gardens, the summer sky, the consciousness of Bertha's arm being within mine, all vanished, and I seemed to be suddenly in darkness, out of which there gradually broke a dim fire-light, and I felt myself sitting in my father's leather chair in the library at home. I knew the fireplace — the dogs for the wood-fire — the black marble chimney-piece with the white marble medallion of the dying Cleopatra in the centre. Intense and hopeless misery was pressing on my soul; the light became stronger, for Bertha was entering with a candle in her hand — Bertha, my wife — with cruel eyes, with green jewels and green leaves on her white ball-dress; every hateful thought within her present to me. . . . "Madman, idiot! why don't you kill yourself, then?" It was a moment of hell. I saw into her pitiless soul — saw its barren worldliness, its scorching hate — and felt it clothe me round like an air I was obliged to breathe. She came with her candle and stood over me with a bitter smile of contempt; I saw the great emerald brooch on her bosom, a studded serpent with diamond eyes. I shuddered — I despised this woman with the barren soul and mean thoughts; but I felt helpless before her, as if she clutched my bleeding heart, and would clutch it till the last drop of life-blood ebbed away. She was my wife, and we hated each other. Gradually the hearth, the dim library, the candle-light disappeared — seemed to melt away into a background of light, the green serpent with the diamond eyes remaining a dark image on the retina. Then I had a sense of my eyelids quivering, and the living daylight broke in upon me; I saw gardens and heard voices. I was seated on the steps of the Belvedere Terrace, and my friends were round me.

29

The tumult of mind into which I was thrown by this hideous vision made me ill for several days, and prolonged our stay at Vienna. I shuddered with horror as the scene recurred to me; and it recurred constantly, with all its minutiae, as if they had been burnt into my memory; and yet, such is the madness of the human heart under the influence of its immediate desires, I felt a wild hell-braving joy that Bertha was to be mine; for the fulfilment of my former prevision concerning her first appearance before me, left me little hope that this last hideous glimpse of the future was the mere diseased play of my own mind, and had no relation to external realities. One thing alone I looked towards as a possible means of casting doubt on my terrible conviction — the discovery that my vision of Prague had been false — and Prague was the next city on our route.

Meanwhile, I was no sooner in Bertha's society again, than I was as completely under her sway as before. What if I saw into the heart of Bertha, the matured woman — Bertha, my wife? Bertha, the *girl*, was a fascinating secret to me still: I trembled under her touch; I felt the witchery of her presence; I yearned to be assured of her love. The fear of poison is feeble against the sense of thirst. Nay, I was just as jealous of my brother as before — just as much irritated by his small patronising ways; for my pride, my diseased sensibility, were there as they had always been, and winced as inevitably under every offence as my eye winced from an intruding mote. The future, even when brought within the compass of feeling by a vision that made me shudder, had still no more than the force of an idea, compared with the force of present emotion — of my love for Bertha, of my dislike and jealousy towards my brother.

It is an old story, that men sell themselves to the tempter, and sign a bond with their blood, because it is only to take effect at a distant day; then rush on to snatch the cup their souls thirst after with an impulse not the less savage because there is a dark shadow beside them for evermore. There is no short cut, no patent tram-road, to wisdom: after all the centuries of invention, the soul's path lies through the thorny wilderness which must be still trodden in solitude, with bleeding feet, with sobs for help, as it was trodden by them of old time.

My mind speculated eagerly on the means by which I should become my brother's successful rival, for I was still too timid, in my ignorance of Bertha's actual feeling, to venture on any step that would urge from her an avowal of it. I thought I should gain confidence even for this, if my vision of Prague proved to have been veracious; and yet, the horror of that certitude! Behind the slim girl Bertha, whose words and looks I watched for, whose touch was bliss, there stood continually that Bertha with the fuller form, the harder eyes, the more rigid mouth, — with the barren selfish soul laid bare; no longer a fascinating secret, but a measured fact, urging itself perpetually on my unwilling sight. Are you unable to give me your sympathy

— you who read this? Are you unable to imagine this double consciousness at work within me, flowing on like two parallel streams which never mingle their waters and blend into a common hue? Yet you must have known something of the presentiments that spring from an insight at war with passion; and my visions were only like presentiments intensified to horror. You have known the powerlessness of ideas before the might of impulse; and my visions, when once they had passed into memory, were mere ideas — pale shadows that beckoned in vain, while my hand was grasped by the living and the loved.

In after-days I thought with bitter regret that if I had foreseen something more or something different — if instead of that hideous vision which poisoned the passion it could not destroy, or if even along with it I could have had a foreshadowing of that moment when I looked on my brother's face for the last time, some softening influence would have been shed over my feeling towards him: pride and hatred would surely have been subdued into pity, and the record of those hidden sins would have been shortened. But this is one of the vain thoughts with which we men flatter ourselves. We try to believe that the egoism within us would have easily been melted, and that it was only the narrowness of our knowledge which hemmed in our generosity, our awe, our human piety, and hindered them from submerging our hard indifference to the sensations and emotions of our fellow. Our tenderness and self-renunciation seem strong when our egoism has had its day—when, after our mean striving for a triumph that is to be another's loss, the triumph comes suddenly, and we shudder at it, because it is held out by the chill hand of death.

Our arrival in Prague happened at night, and I was glad of this, for it seemed like a deferring of a terribly decisive moment, to be in the city for hours without seeing it. As we were not to remain long in Prague, but to go on speedily to Dresden, it was proposed that we should drive out the next morning and take a general view of the place, as well as visit some of its specially interesting spots, before the heat became oppressive—for we were in August, and the season was hot and dry. But it happened that the ladies were rather late at their morning toilet, and to my father's politely-repressed but perceptible annoyance, we were not in the carriage till the morning was far advanced. I thought with a sense of relief, as we entered the Jews' quarter, where we were to visit the old synagogue, that we should be kept in this flat, shut-up part of the city, until we should all be too tired and too warm to go farther, and so we should return without seeing more than the streets through which we had already passed. That would give me another day's suspense—suspense, the only form in which a fearful spirit knows the solace of hope. But, as I stood under the blackened, groined arches of that old synagogue, made dimly visible by the seven thin candles in the sacred lamp, while our Jewish cicerone reached down the Book of the Law, and read to us in its ancient tongue, — I felt a shuddering impression that this strange building, with its shrunken lights, this surviving withered remnant of medieval Judaism, was of a piece with my vision. Those darkened dusty Christian saints, with their loftier arches and their larger candles, needed the consolatory scorn with which they might point to a more shrivelled death-in-life than their own.

As I expected, when we left the Jews' quarter the elders of our party wished to return to the hotel. But now, instead of rejoicing in this, as I had done beforehand, I felt a sudden overpowering impulse to go on at once to the bridge, and put an end to the suspense I had been wishing to protract. I declared, with unusual decision, that I would get out of the carriage and walk on alone; they might return without me. My father, thinking this merely a sample of my usual "poetic nonsense", objected that I should only do myself harm by walking in the heat; but when I persisted, he said angrily that I might follow my own absurd devices, but that Schmidt (our courier) must go with me. I assented to this, and set off with Schmidt towards the bridge. I had no sooner passed from under the archway of the grand old gate leading on to the bridge, than a trembling seized me, and I turned cold under the mid-day sun; yet I went on; I was in search of something—a small detail which I remembered with special intensity as part of my vision. There it was — the patch of rainbow light on the pavement transmitted through a lamp in the shape of a star.

CHAPTER II

BEFORE the autumn was at an end, and while the brown leaves still stood thick on the beeches in our park, my brother and Bertha were engaged to each other, and it was understood that their marriage was to take place early in the next spring. In spite of the certainty I had felt from that moment on the bridge at Prague, that Bertha would one day be my wife, my constitutional timidity and distrust had continued to benumb me, and the words in which I had sometimes premeditated a confession of my love, had died away unuttered. The same conflict had gone on within me as before — the longing for an assurance of love from Bertha's lips, the dread lest a word of contempt and denial should fall upon me like a corrosive acid. What was the conviction of a distant necessity to me? I trembled under a present glance, I hungered after a present joy, I was clogged and chilled by a present fear. And so the days passed on: I witnessed Bertha's engagement and heard her marriage discussed as if I were under a conscious nightmare — knowing it was a

35

dream that would vanish, but feeling stifled under the grasp of hard-clutching fingers.

When I was not in Bertha's presence — and I was with her very often, for she continued to treat me with a playful patronage that wakened no jealousy in my brother — I spent my time chiefly in wandering, in strolling, or taking long rides while the daylight lasted, and then shutting myself up with my unread books; for books had lost the power of chaining my attention. My self-consciousness was heightened to that pitch of intensity in which our own emotions take the form of a drama which urges itself imperatively on our contemplation, and we begin to weep, less under the sense of our suffering than at the thought of it. I felt a sort of pitying anguish over the pathos of my own lot: the lot of a being finely organised for pain, but with hardly any fibres that responded to pleasure — to whom the idea of future evil robbed the present of its joy, and for whom the idea of future good did not still the uneasiness of a present yearning or a present dread. I went dumbly through that stage of the poet's suffering, in which he feels the delicious pang of utterance, and makes an image of his sorrows.

I was left entirely without remonstrance concerning this dreamy wayward life: I knew my father's thought about me: "That lad will never be good for anything in life: he may waste his years in an insignificant way on the income that falls to him: I shall not trouble myself about a career for him."

One mild morning in the beginning of November, it happened that I was standing outside the portico patting lazy old Caesar, a Newfoundland almost blind with age, the only dog that ever took any notice of me — for the very dogs shunned me, and fawned on the happier people about me — when the groom brought up my brother's horse which was to carry him to the hunt, and my brother himself appeared at the door, florid, broad-chested, and self-complacent, feeling what a good-natured fellow he was not to behave insolently to us all on the strength of his great advantages.

"Latimer, old boy," he said to me in a tone of compassionate cordiality, "what a pity it is you don't have a run with the hounds now and then! The finest thing in the world for low spirits!"

"Low spirits!" I thought bitterly, as he rode away; "that is the sort of phrase with which coarse, narrow natures like yours think to describe experience of which you can know no more than your horse knows. It is to such as you that the good of this world falls: ready dullness, healthy selfishness, good-tempered conceit — these are the keys to happiness."

The quick thought came, that my selfishness was even stronger than his — it was only a suffering selfishness instead of an enjoying one. But then, again, my exasperating insight into Alfred's self-complacent soul, his freedom from all the doubts and fears, the unsatisfied yearnings, the exquisite tortures of sensitiveness, that had made the web of my life, seemed to absolve me from all bonds towards him. This man needed no pity, no love; those fine influences would have been as little felt by him as the delicate white mist is felt by the rock it caresses. There was no evil in store for *him*: if he was not to marry Bertha, it would be because he had found a lot pleasanter to himself.

Mr Filmore's house lay not more than half a mile beyond our own gates, and whenever I knew my brother was gone in another direction, I went there for the chance of finding Bertha at home. Later on in the day I walked thither. By a rare accident she was alone, and we walked out in the grounds together, for she seldom went on foot beyond the trimly-swept gravel-walks. I remember what a beautiful sylph she looked to me as the low November sun shone on her blond hair, and she tripped along teasing me with her usual light banter, to which I listened half fondly, half moodily; it was all the sign Bertha's mysterious inner self ever made to me. To-day perhaps the moodiness predominated, for I had not yet shaken off the access of jealous hate which my brother had raised in me by his parting patronage. Suddenly I interrupted and startled her by saying, almost fiercely, "Bertha, how can you love Alfred?"

She looked at me with surprise for a moment, but soon her light smile came again, and she answered sarcastically, "Why do you suppose I love him?"

"How can you ask that, Bertha?"

"What! your wisdom thinks I must love the man I'm going to marry? The most unpleasant thing in the world. I should quarrel with him; I should be jealous of him; our *ménage* would be conducted in a very ill-bred manner. A little quiet contempt contributes greatly to the elegance of life."

"Bertha, that is not your real feeling. Why do you delight in trying to deceive me by inventing such cynical speeches?"

"I need never take the trouble of invention in order to deceive you, my small Tasso" — (that was the mocking name she usually gave me). "The easiest way to deceive a poet is to tell him the truth."

She was testing the validity of her epigram in a daring way, and for a moment the shadow of my vision — the Bertha whose soul was no secret to me — passed between me and the radiant girl, the playful sylph whose feelings were a fascinating mystery. I suppose I must have shuddered, or betrayed in some other way my momentary chill of horror.

"Tasso!" she said, seizing my wrist, and peeping round into my face, "are you really beginning to discern what a heartless girl I am? Why, you are not half the poet I thought you were; you are actually capable of believing the truth about me."

The shadow passed from between us, and was no longer the object nearest to me. The girl whose light fingers grasped me, whose elfish charming face looked into

39

mine — who, I thought, was betraying an interest in my feelings that she would not have directly avowed, — this warm-breathing presence again possessed my senses and imagination like a returning syren melody which had been overpowered for an instant by the roar of threatening waves. It was a moment as delicious to me as the waking up to a consciousness of youth after a dream of middle age. I forgot everything but my passion, and said with swimming eyes —

"Bertha, shall you love me when we are first married? I wouldn't mind if you really loved me only for a little while."

Her look of astonishment, as she loosed my hand and started away from me recalled me to a sense of my strange, my criminal indiscretion.

"Forgive me," I said, hurriedly, as soon as I could speak again; "I did not know what I was saying."

"Ah, Tasso's mad fit has come on, I see," she answered quietly, for she had recovered herself sooner than I had. "Let him go home and keep his head cool. I must go in, for the sun is setting."

I left her — full of indignation against myself. I had let slip words which, if she reflected on them, might rouse in her a suspicion of my abnormal mental condition — a suspicion which of all things I dreaded. And besides that, I was ashamed of the apparent baseness I had committed in uttering them to my brother's betrothed wife. I wandered home slowly, entering our park through a private gate instead of by the lodges. As I approached the house, I saw a man dashing off at full speed from the stable-yard across the park. Had any accident happened at home? No; perhaps it was only one of my father's peremptory business errands that required this headlong haste. Nevertheless I quickened my pace without any distinct motive, and was soon at the house. I will not dwell on the scene I found there. My brother was dead—had been pitched from his horse, and killed on the spot by a concussion of the brain.

I went up to the room where he lay, and where my father was seated beside him with a look of rigid despair. I had shunned my father more than any one since our return home, for the radical antipathy between our natures made my insight into his inner self a constant affliction to me. But now, as I went up to him, and stood beside him in sad silence, I felt the presence of a new element that blended us as we had never been blent before. My father had been one of the most successful men in the money-getting world: he had had no sentimental sufferings, no illness. The heaviest trouble that had befallen him was the death of his first wife. But he married my mother soon after; and I remember he seemed exactly the same, to my keen childish observation, the week after her death as before. But now, at last, a sorrow had come—the sorrow of old age, which suffers the more from the crushing of its pride and its hopes, in proportion as the pride and hope are narrow and prosaic.

His son was to have been married soon — would probably have stood for the borough at the next election. That son's existence was the best motive that could be alleged for making new purchases of land every year to round off the estate. It is a dreary thing to live on doing the same things year after year, without knowing why we do them. Perhaps the tragedy of disappointed youth and passion is less piteous than the tragedy of disappointed age and worldliness.

As I saw into the desolation of my father's heart, I felt a movement of deep pity towards him, which was the beginning of a new affection — an affection that grew and strengthened in spite of the strange bitterness with which he regarded me in the first month or two after my brother's death. If it had not been for the softening influence of my compassion for him — the first deep compassion I had ever felt — I should have been stung by the perception that my father transferred the inheritance of an eldest son to me with a mortified sense that fate had compelled him to the unwelcome course of caring for me as an important being. It was only in spite of himself that he began to think of me with anxious regard. There is hardly any neglected child for whom death has made vacant a more favoured place, who will not understand what I mean.

Gradually, however, my new deference to his wishes, the effect of that patience which was born of my pity for him, won upon his affection, and he began to please himself with the endeavour to make me fill my brother's place as fully as my feebler personality would admit. I saw that the prospect which by-and-by presented itself of my becoming Bertha's husband was welcome to him, and he even contemplated in my case what he had not intended in my brother's — that his son and daughter-in-law should make one household with him. My softened feeling towards my father made this the happiest time I had known since childhood; — these last months in which I retained the delicious illusion of loving Bertha, of longing and doubting and hoping that she might love me. She behaved with a certain new consciousness and distance towards me after my brother's death; and I too was under a double constraint — that of delicacy towards my brother's memory, and of anxiety as to the impression my abrupt words had left on her mind. But the additional screen this mutual reserve erected between us only brought me more completely under her power: no matter how empty the adytum, so that the veil be thick enough. So absolute is our soul's need of something hidden and uncertain for the maintenance of that doubt and hope and effort which are the breath of its life, that if the whole future were laid bare to us beyond to-day, the interest of all mankind would be bent on the hours that lie between; we should pant after the uncertainties of our one morning and our one afternoon; we should rush fiercely to the Exchange for our last possibility of speculation, of success, of disappointment; we should have a glut of political prophets foretelling a crisis or a no-crisis within the only twenty-four hours left open to prophecy. Conceive the condition of the human mind if all propositions whatsoever were self-evident except one, which was to become self-evident at the close of the summer's day, but in the meantime might be the subject of question, of hypothesis, of debate. Art and philosophy, literature and science, would fasten like bees on that one proposition which had the honey of probability in it, and be the more eager because their enjoyment would end with sunset. Our impulses, our spiritual activities, no more adjust themselves to the idea of their future nullity, than the beating of our heart, or the irritability of our muscles.

Bertha, the slim, fair-haired girl, whose present thoughts and emotions were an enigma to me amidst the fatiguing obviousness of the other minds around me, was as absorbing to me as a single unknown to-day — as a single hypothetic proposition to remain problematic till sunset; and all the cramped, hemmed-in belief and disbelief, trust and distrust, of my nature, welled out in this one narrow channel.

And she made me believe that she loved me. Without ever quitting her tone of *badinage* and playful superiority, she intoxicated me with the sense that I was necessary to her, that she was never at ease unless I was near her, submitting to her playful tyranny. It costs a woman so little effort to besot us in this way! A half-repressed word, a moment's unexpected silence, even an easy fit of petulance on our account, will serve us as *hashish* for a long while. Out of the subtlest web of scarcely perceptible signs, she set me weaving the fancy that she had always unconsciously loved me better than Alfred, but that, with the ignorant fluttered sensibility of a young girl, she had been imposed on by the charm that lay for her in the distinction of being admired and chosen by a man who made so brilliant a figure in the world as my brother. She satirised herself in a very graceful way for her vanity and ambition. What was it to me that I had the light of my wretched prevision on the fact that now it was I who possessed at least all but the personal part of my brother's advantages? Our sweet illusions are half of them conscious illusions, like effects of colour that we know to be made up of tinsel, broken glass, and rags.

We were married eighteen months after Alfred's death, one cold, clear morning in April, when there came hail and sunshine both together; and Bertha, in her white silk and pale-green leaves, and the pale hues of her hair and face, looked like the spirit of the morning. My father was happier than he had thought of being again: my marriage, he felt sure, would complete the desirable modification of my character, and make me practical and worldly enough to take my place in society among sane men. For he delighted in Bertha's tact and acuteness, and felt sure she would be mistress of me, and make me what she chose: I was only twenty-one, and madly in love with her. Poor father! He kept that hope a little while after our first year of marriage, and it was not quite extinct when paralysis came and saved him from utter disappointment.

I shall hurry through the rest of my story, not dwelling so much as I have hitherto done on my inward experience. When people are well known to each other, they talk rather of what befalls them externally, leaving their feelings and sentiments to be inferred.

We lived in a round of visits for some time after our return home, giving splendid dinner-parties, and making a sensation in our neighbourhood by the new lustre of our equipage, for my father had reserved this display of his increased wealth for the period of his son's marriage; and we gave our acquaintances liberal opportunity for remarking that it was a pity I made so poor a figure as an heir and a bridegroom. The nervous fatigue of this existence, the insincerities and platitudes which I had to live through twice over — through my inner and outward sense — would have been maddening to me, if I had not had that sort of intoxicated callousness which came from the delights of a first passion. A bride and bridegroom, surrounded by all the appliances of wealth, hurried through the day by the whirl of society, filling their solitary moments with hastily-snatched caresses, are prepared for their future life together as the novice is prepared for the cloister — by experiencing its utmost contrast.

Through all these crowded excited months, Bertha's inward self remained shrouded from me, and I still read her thoughts only through the language of her lips and demeanour: I had still the human interest of wondering whether what I did and said pleased her, of longing to hear a word of affection, of giving a delicious exaggeration of meaning to her smile. But I was conscious of a growing difference in her manner towards me; sometimes strong enough to be called haughty coldness, cutting and chilling me as the hail had done that came across the sunshine on our marriage morning; sometimes only perceptible in the dexterous avoidance of a *tête-à-tête* walk or dinner to which I had been looking forward. I had been deeply pained by this — had even felt a sort of crushing of the heart, from the sense that my brief day of happiness was near its setting; but still I remained dependent on Bertha, eager for the last rays of a bliss that would soon be gone for ever, hoping and watching for some after-glow more beautiful from the impending night.

I remember — how should I not remember? — the time when that dependence and hope utterly left me, when the sadness I had felt in Bertha's growing estrangement became a joy that I looked back upon with longing, as a man might look back on the last pains in a paralysed limb. It was just after the close of my father's last illness, which had necessarily withdrawn us from society and thrown us more upon each other. It was the evening of my father's death. On that evening the veil which had shrouded Bertha's soul from me — had made me find in her alone among my fellow-beings the blessed possibility of mystery, and doubt, and expectation— was first withdrawn. Perhaps it was the first day since the beginning of my passion for her, in which that passion was completely neutralised by the presence of an absorbing feeling of another kind. I had been watching by my father's deathbed: I had been witnessing the last fitful yearning glance his soul had cast back on the spent inheritance of life— the last faint consciousness of love he had gathered from the pressure of my hand. What are all our personal loves when we have been sharing in that supreme agony? In the first moments when we come away from the presence of death, every other relation to the living is merged, to our feeling, in the great relation of a common nature and a common destiny.

In that state of mind I joined Bertha in her private sitting-room. She was seated in a leaning posture on a settee, with her back towards the door; the great rich coils of her pale blond hair surmounting her small neck, visible above the back of the settee. I remember, as I closed the door behind me, a cold tremulousness seizing me, and a vague sense of being hated and lonely— vague and strong, like a presentiment. I know how I looked at that moment, for I saw myself in Bertha's thought as she lifted her cutting grey eyes, and looked at me: a miserable ghost-seer, surrounded by phantoms in the noon-day, trembling under a breeze when the leaves were still, without appetite for the common objects of human desire, but pining after the moonbeams. We were front to front with each other, and judged each other. The terrible moment of complete illumination had come to me, and I saw that the darkness had hidden no landscape from me, but only a blank prosaic wall: from that evening forth, through the sickening years which followed, I saw all round the narrow room of this woman's soul — saw petty artifice and mere negation where I had delighted to believe in coy sensibilities and in wit at war with latent feeling — saw the light floating vanities of the girl defining themselves into the systematic coquetry, the scheming selfishness, of the woman — saw repulsion and antipathy harden into cruel hatred, giving pain only for the sake of wreaking itself.

For Bertha too, after her kind, felt the bitterness of disillusion. She had believed that my wild poet's passion for her would make me her slave; and that, being her slave, I should execute her will in all things. With the essential shallowness of a negative, unimaginative nature, she was unable to conceive the fact that sensibilities were anything else than weaknesses. She had thought my weaknesses would put me in her power, and she found them unmanageable forces. Our positions were reversed. Before marriage she had completely mastered my imagination, for she was a secret to me; and I created the unknown thought before which I trembled as if it were hers. But now that her soul was laid open to me, now that I was compelled to share the privacy of her motives, to follow all the petty devices that preceded her words and acts, she found herself powerless with me, except to produce in me the chill shudder of repulsion — powerless, because I could be acted on by no lever within her reach. I was dead to worldly ambitions, to social vanities, to all the incentives within the compass of her narrow imagination, and I lived under influences utterly invisible to her.

She was really pitiable to have such a husband, and so all the world thought. A graceful, brilliant woman, like Bertha, who smiled on morning callers, made a figure in ball-rooms, and was capable of that light repartee which, from such a woman, is accepted as wit, was secure of carrying off all sympathy from a husband who was sickly, abstracted, and, as some suspected, crack-brained. Even the servants in our house gave her the balance of their regard and pity. For there were no audible quarrels between us; our alienation, our repulsion from each other, lay within the silence of our own hearts; and if the mistress went out a great deal, and seemed to dislike the master's society, was it not natural, poor thing? The master was odd. I was kind and just to my dependants, but I excited in them a shrinking, half-contemptuous pity; for this class of men and women are but slightly determined in their estimate of others by general considerations, or even experience, of character. They judge of persons as they judge of coins, and value those who pass current at a high rate.

After a time I interfered so little with Bertha's habits, that it might seem wonderful how her hatred towards me

could grow so intense and active as it did. But she had
begun to suspect, by some involuntary betrayals of mine,
that there was an abnormal power of penetration in me
— that fitfully, at least, I was strangely cognisant of her
thoughts and intentions, and she began to be haunted by
a terror of me, which alternated every now and then with
defiance. She meditated continually how the incubus
could be shaken off her life — how she could be freed from
this hateful bond to a being whom she at once despised as
an imbecile, and dreaded as an inquisitor. For a long
while she lived in the hope that my evident wretchedness
would drive me to the commission of suicide; but suicide
was not in my nature. I was too completely swayed
by the sense that I was in the grasp of unknown forces,
to believe in my power of self-release. Towards my own
destiny I had become entirely passive; for my one ardent
desire had spent itself, and impulse no longer predominated over knowledge. For this reason I never thought of
taking any steps towards a complete separation, which
would have made our alienation evident to the world.
Why should I rush for help to a new course, when I was
only suffering from the consequences of a deed which had
been the act of my intensest will? That would have been
the logic of one who had desires to gratify, and I had no
desires. But Bertha and I lived more and more aloof from
each other. The rich find it easy to live married
and apart.

That course of our life which I have indicated in a few

sentences filled the space of years. So much misery — so slow and hideous a growth of hatred and sin, may be compressed into a sentence! And men judge of each other's lives through this summary medium. They epitomise the experience of their fellow-mortal, and pronounce judgment on him in neat syntax, and feel themselves wise and virtuous — conquerors over the temptations they define in well-selected predicates. Seven years of wretchedness glide glibly over the lips of the man who has never counted them out in moments of chill disappointment, of head and heart throbbings, or dread and vain wrestling, of remorse and despair. We learn *words* by rote, but not their meaning; *that* must be paid for with our life-blood, and printed in the subtle fibres of our nerves.

But I will hasten to finish my story. Brevity is justified at once to those who readily understand, and to those who will never understand.

Some years after my father's death, I was sitting by the dim firelight in my library one January evening — sitting in the leather chair that used to be my father's — when Bertha appeared at the door, with a candle in her hand, and advanced towards me. I knew the ball-dress she had on — the white ball-dress, with the green jewels, shone upon by the light of the wax candle which lit up the medallion of the dying Cleopatra on the mantelpiece. Why did she come to me before going out? I had not seen her in the library, which was my habitual place, for months. Why did she stand before me with the candle in her hand, with her cruel contemptuous eyes fixed on me, and the glittering serpent, like a familiar demon, on her breast? For a moment I thought this fulfilment of my vision at Vienna marked some dreadful crisis in my fate, but I saw nothing in Bertha's mind, as she stood before me, except scorn for the look of overwhelming misery with which I sat before her. . . . "Fool, idiot, why don't you kill yourself, then?" —that was her thought. But at length her thoughts reverted to her errand, and she spoke aloud. The apparently indifferent nature of the errand seemed to make a ridiculous anticlimax to my prevision and my agitation.

"I have had to hire a new maid. Fletcher is going to be married, and she wants me to ask you to let her husband have the public-house and farm at Molton. I wish him to have it. You must give the promise now, because Fletcher is going tomorrow morning—and quickly, because I'm in a hurry."

"Very well; you may promise her," I said, indifferently, and Bertha swept out of the library again.

I always shrank from the sight of a new person, and all the more when it was a person whose mental life was likely to weary my reluctant insight with worldly ignorant trivialities. But I shrank especially from the sight of this new maid, because her advent had been announced to me at a moment to which I could not cease to attach some fatality: I had a vague dread that I should find her mixed up with the dreary drama of my life— that some new sickening vision would reveal her to me as an evil genius. When at last I did unavoidably meet her, the vague dread was changed into definite disgust. She was a tall, wiry, dark-eyed woman, this Mrs Archer, with a face handsome enough to give her coarse, hard nature the odious finish of bold, self-confident coquetry. That was enough to make me avoid her, quite apart from the contemptuous feeling with which she contemplated me. I seldom saw her; but I perceived that she rapidly became a favourite with her mistress, and, after the lapse of eight or nine months, I began to be aware that there had arisen in Bertha's mind towards this woman a mingled feeling of fear and dependence, and that this feeling was associated with ill-defined images of candle-light scenes in her dressing-room, and the locking-up of something in Bertha's cabinet. My interviews with my wife had become so brief and so rarely solitary, that I had no opportunity of perceiving these images in her mind with more definiteness. The recollections of the past become contracted in the rapidity of thought till they sometimes bear hardly a more distinct resemblance to the external reality than the forms of an oriental alphabet to the objects that suggested them.

Besides, for the last year or more a modification had been going forward in my mental condition, and was growing more and more marked. My insight into the minds of those around me was becoming dimmer and more fitful, and the ideas that crowded my double consciousness became less and less dependent on any personal contact. All that was personal in me seemed to be suffering a gradual death, so that I was losing the organ through which the personal agitations and projects of others could affect me. But along with this relief from wearisome insight, there was a new development of what I concluded — as I have since found rightly — to be a prevision of external scenes. It was as if the relation between me and my fellow-men was more and more deadened, and my relation to what we call the inanimate was quickened into new life. The more I lived apart from society, and in proportion as my wretchedness subsided from the violent throb of agonised passion into the dulness of habitual pain, the more frequent and vivid became such visions as that I had had of Prague — of strange cities, of sandy plains, of gigantic ruins, of midnight skies with strange bright constellations, of mountain-passes, of grassy nooks flecked with the afternoon sunshine through the boughs: I was in the midst of such scenes, and in all of them one presence seemed to weigh on me in all these mighty shapes — the presence of something unknown and pitiless. For continual suffering had annihilated religious faith within me: to the utterly miserable — the unloving and the unloved — there is no religion possible, no worship but a worship of devils. And beyond all these, and continually recurring, was the vision of my death — the pangs, the suffocation, the last struggle, when life would be grasped at in vain.

Things were in this state near the end of the seventh year. I had become entirely free from insight, from my abnormal cognisance of any other consciousness than my own, and instead of intruding involuntarily into the world of other minds, was living continually in my own solitary future. Bertha was aware that I was greatly changed. To my surprise she had of late seemed to seek opportunities of remaining in my society, and had cultivated that kind of distant yet familiar talk which is customary between a husband and wife who live in polite and irrevocable alienation. I bore this with languid submission, and without feeling enough interest in her motives to be roused into keen observation; yet I could not help perceiving something triumphant and excited in her carriage and the expression of her face — something too subtle to express itself in words or tones, but giving one the idea that she lived in a state of expectation or hopeful suspense. My chief feeling was satisfaction that her inner self was once more shut out from me; and I almost revelled for the moment in the absent melancholy that made me answer her at cross purposes, and betray utter ignorance of what she had been saying. I remember well the look and the smile with which she one day said, after a mistake of this kind on my part: "I used to think you were a clairvoyant, and that was the reason why you were so bitter against other clairvoyants, wanting to keep your monopoly; but I see now you have become rather duller than the rest of the world."

I said nothing in reply. It occurred to me that her recent obtrusion of herself upon me might have been prompted by the wish to test my power of detecting some of her secrets; but I let the thought drop again at once: her motives and her deeds had no interest for me, and whatever pleasures she might be seeking, I had no wish to balk her. There was still pity in my soul for every living thing, and Bertha was living—was surrounded with possibilities of misery.

Just at this time there occurred an event which roused me somewhat from my inertia, and gave me an interest in the passing moment that I had thought impossible for me. It was a visit from Charles Meunier, who had written me word that he was coming to England for relaxation from too strenuous labour, and would like to see me. Meunier had now a European reputation; but his letter to me expressed that keen remembrance of an early regard, an early debt of sympathy, which is inseparable from nobility of character: and I too felt as if his presence would be to me like a transient resurrection into a happier pre-existence.

He came, and as far as possible, I renewed our old pleasure of making *tête-à-tête* excursions, though, instead of mountains and glaciers and the wide blue lake, we had to content ourselves with mere slopes and ponds and artificial plantations. The years had changed us both, but with what different result! Meunier was now a brilliant figure in society, to whom elegant women pretended to listen, and whose acquaintance was boasted of by noblemen ambitious of brains. He repressed with the utmost delicacy all betrayal of the shock which I am sure he must have received from our meeting, or of a desire to penetrate into my condition and circumstances, and sought by the utmost exertion of his charming social powers to make our reunion agreeable. Bertha was much struck by the unexpected fascinations of a visitor whom she had expected to find presentable only on the score of his celebrity, and put forth all her coquetries and accomplishments. Apparently she succeeded in attracting his admiration, for his manner towards her was attentive and flattering. The effect of his presence on me was so benignant, especially in those renewals of our old *tête-à-tête* wanderings, when he poured forth to me wonderful narratives of his professional experience, that more than once, when his talk turned on the psychological relations of disease, the thought crossed my mind that, if his stay with me were long enough, I might possibly bring myself to tell this man the secrets of my lot. Might there not lie some remedy for *me*, too, in his science? Might there not at least lie some comprehension and sympathy ready for me in his large and susceptible mind? But the thought only flickered feebly now and then, and died out before it could become a wish. The horror I had of again breaking in on the privacy of another soul, made me, by an irrational instinct, draw the shroud of concealment more closely around my own, as we automatically perform the gesture we feel to be wanting in another.

When Meunier's visit was approaching its conclusion, there happened an event which caused some excitement in our household, owing to the surprisingly strong effect it appeared to produce on Bertha — on Bertha, the self-possessed, who usually seemed inaccessible to feminine agitations, and did even her hate in a self-restrained hygienic manner. This event was the sudden illness of her maid, Mrs Archer. I have reserved to this moment the mention of a circumstance which had forced itself on my notice shortly before Meunier's arrival, namely, that there had been some quarrel between Bertha and this maid, apparently during a visit to a distant family, in which she had accompanied her mistress. I had overheard Archer speaking in a tone of bitter insolence, which I should have thought an adequate reason for immediate dismissal. No dismissal followed; on the contrary, Bertha seemed to be silently putting up with personal inconveniences from the exhibitions of this woman's temper. I was the more astonished to observe that her illness seemed a cause of strong solicitude to Bertha; that she was at the bedside night and day, and would allow no one else to officiate as head-nurse. It happened that our family doctor was out on a holiday, an accident which made Meunier's presence in the house doubly welcome, and he apparently entered into the case with an interest which seemed so much stronger than the ordinary professional feeling, that one day when he had fallen into a long fit of silence after visiting her, I said to him—

"Is this a very peculiar case of disease, Meunier?"

"No," he answered, "it is an attack of peritonitis, which will be fatal, but which does not differ physically from many other cases that have come under my observation. But I'll tell you what I have on my mind. I want to make an experiment on this woman, if you will give me permission. It can do her no harm—will give her no pain—for I shall not make it until life is extinct to all purposes of sensation. I want to try the effect of transfusing blood into her arteries after the heart has ceased to beat for some minutes. I have tried the experiment again and again with animals that have died of this disease, with astounding results, and I want to try it on a human subject. I have the small tubes necessary, in a case I have with me, and the rest of the apparatus could be prepared readily. I should use my own blood—take it from my own arm. This woman won't live through the night, I'm convinced, and I want you to promise me your assistance in making the experiment. I can't do without another hand, but it would perhaps not be well to call in a medical assistant from among your provincial doctors. A disagreeable foolish version of the thing might get abroad."

"Have you spoken to my wife on the subject?" I said, "because she appears to be peculiarly sensitive about this woman: she has been a favourite maid."

"To tell you the truth," said Meunier, "I don't want her to know about it. There are always insuperable difficulties with women in these matters, and the effect on the supposed dead body may be startling. You and I will sit up together, and be in readiness. When certain symptoms appear I shall take you in, and at the right moment we must manage to get every one else out of the room."

I need not give our farther conversation on the subject. He entered very fully into the details, and overcame my repulsion from them, by exciting in me a mingled awe and curiosity concerning the possible results of his experiment.

We prepared everything, and he instructed me in my part as assistant. He had not told Bertha of his absolute conviction that Archer would not survive through the night, and endeavoured to persuade her to leave the patient and take a night's rest. But she was obstinate, suspecting the fact that death was at hand, and supposing that he wished merely to save her nerves. She refused to leave the sick-room. Meunier and I sat up together in the library, he making frequent visits to the sick-room, and returning with the information that the case was taking precisely the course he expected. Once he said to me, "Can you imagine any cause of ill feeling this woman has against her mistress, who is so devoted to her?"

"I think there was some misunderstanding between them before her illness. Why do you ask?"

"Because I have observed for the last five or six hours

— since, I fancy, she has lost all hope of recovery — there seems a strange prompting in her to say something which pain and failing strength forbid her to utter; and there is a look of hideous meaning in her eyes, which she turns continually towards her mistress. In this disease the mind often remains singularly clear to the last."

"I am not surprised at an indication of malevolent feeling in her," I said. "She is a woman who has always inspired me with distrust and dislike, but she managed to insinuate herself into her mistress's favour." He was silent after this, looking at the fire with an air of absorption, till he went upstairs again. He stayed away longer than usual, and on returning, said to me quietly, "Come now."

I followed him to the chamber where death was hovering. The dark hangings of the large bed made a background that gave a strong relief to Bertha's pale face as she saw me enter, and then looked at Meunier with an expression of angry inquiry; but he lifted up his hand as if to impose silence, while he fixed his glance on the dying woman and felt her pulse. The face was pinched and ghastly, a cold perspiration was on the forehead, and the eyelids were lowered so as almost to conceal the large dark eyes. After a minute or two, Meunier walked round to the other side of the bed where Bertha stood, and with his usual air of gentle politeness towards her begged her to leave the patient under our care — everything should be done for her — she was no longer in a state to be conscious of an affectionate presence. Bertha was hesitating, apparently almost willing to believe his assurance and to comply. She looked round at the ghastly dying face, as if to read the confirmation of that assurance, when for a moment the lowered eyelids were raised again, and it seemed as if the eyes were looking towards Bertha, but blankly. A shudder passed through Bertha's frame, and she returned to her station near the pillow, tacitly implying that she would not leave the room.

The eyelids were lifted no more. Once I looked at Bertha as she watched the face of the dying one. She wore a rich *peignoir*, and her blond hair was half covered by a lace cap: in her attire she was, as always, an elegant woman, fit to figure in a picture of modern aristocratic life: but I asked myself how that face of hers could ever have seemed to me the face of a woman born of woman, with memories of childhood, capable of pain, needing to be fondled? The features at that moment seemed so preternaturally sharp, the eyes were so hard and eager — she looked like a cruel immortal, finding her spiritual feast in the agonies of a dying race. For across those hard features there came something like a flash when the last hour had been breathed out, and we all felt that the dark veil had completely fallen. What secret was there between Bertha and this woman? I turned my eyes from her with a horrible dread lest my insight should return, and I should be obliged to see what had been breeding about two unloving women's hearts. I felt that Bertha had been watching for the moment of death as the sealing of her secret: I thanked Heaven it could remain sealed for me.

Meunier said quietly, "She is gone." He then gave his arm to Bertha, and she submitted to be led out of the room.

I suppose it was at her order that two female attendants came into the room, and dismissed the younger one who had been present before. When they entered, Meunier had already opened the artery in the long thin neck that lay rigid on the pillow, and I dismissed them, ordering them to remain at a distance till we rang: the doctor, I said, had an operation to perform — he was not sure about the death. For the next twenty minutes I forgot everything but Meunier and the experiment in which he was so absorbed, that I think his senses would have been closed against all sounds or sights which had no relation to it. It was my task at first to keep up the artificial respiration in the body after the transfusion had been effected, but presently Meunier relieved me, and I could see the wondrous slow return of life; the breast began to heave, the inspirations became stronger, the eyelids quivered, and the soul seemed to have returned beneath them. The artificial respiration was withdrawn: still the breathing continued, and there was a movement of the lips.

Just then I heard the handle of the door moving: I suppose Bertha had heard from the women that they had been dismissed: probably a vague fear had arisen in her mind, for she entered with a look of alarm. She came to the foot of the bed and gave a stifled cry.

The dead woman's eyes were wide open, and met hers in full recognition — the recognition of hate. With a sudden strong effort, the hand that Bertha had thought for ever still was pointed towards her, and the haggard face moved. The gasping eager voice said —

"You mean to poison your husband . . . the poison is in the black cabinet . . . I got it for you . . . you laughed at me, and told lies about me behind my back, to make me disgusting . . . because you were jealous . . . are you sorry . . . now?"

The lips continued to murmur, but the sounds were no longer distinct. Soon there was no sound — only a slight movement: the flame had leaped out, and was being extinguished the faster. The wretched woman's heart-strings had been set to hatred and vengeance; the spirit of life had swept the chords for an instant, and was gone again for ever. Great God! Is this what it is to live again . . . to wake up with our unstilled thirst upon us, with our unuttered curses rising to our lips, with our muscles ready to act out their half-committed sins?

Bertha stood pale at the foot of the bed, quivering and helpless, despairing of devices, like a cunning animal whose hiding-places are surrounded by swift-advancing flame. Even Meunier looked paralysed; life for that moment ceased to be a scientific problem to him. As for me, this scene seemed of one texture with the rest of my existence: horror was my familiar, and this new revelation was only like an old pain recurring with new circumstances.

.   .   .   .

Since then Bertha and I have lived apart — she in her own neighbourhood, the mistress of half our wealth, I as a wanderer in foreign countries, until I came to this Devonshire nest to die. Bertha lives pitied and admired; for what had I against that charming woman, whom every one but myself could have been happy with? There had been no witness of the scene in the dying room except Meunier, and while Meunier lived his lips were sealed by a promise to me.

Once or twice, weary of wandering, I rested in a favourite spot, and my heart went out towards the men and women and children whose faces were becoming familiar to me: but I was driven away again in terror at the approach of my old insight — driven away to live continually with the one Unknown Presence revealed and yet hidden by the moving curtain of the earth and sky. Till at last disease took hold of me and forced me to rest here — forced me to live in dependence on my servants. And then the curse of insight — of my double consciousness, came again, and has never left me. I know all their narrow thoughts, their feeble regard, their half-wearied pity.

.   .   .   .

It is the 20th of September 1850. I know these figures I have just written, as if they were a long familiar inscription. I have seen them on this page in my desk unnumbered times, when the scene of my dying struggle has opened upon me. . . .

AFTERWORD

Less than three months after the appearance in 1859 of
her first novel, the reverenced and commercially successful *Adam Bede*, George Eliot embarrassed her publishers
by sending them the manuscript of *The Lifted Veil* for
publication in their magazine. John Blackwood and his
brother William found it difficult to reconcile their idea of
the author of the "beautiful most human book"[1] with the
author of this dismal story of clairvoyance, attempted
murder, and ghoulish, quasi-scientific resurrection from
the dead, and nervously rejected the suggestion by George
Henry Lewes — George Eliot's "husband" — that her
name be affixed to it. *The Mill on the Floss* was already
under way: this was to be the *proper* successor to *Adam
Bede*, and it would be imprudent, they felt, to risk
tarnishing the valuable author's prestige by associating it
in the meantime with so unsuitable a production.

The view that *The Lifted Veil* is an aberration has

1. Mrs Carlyle. See *The George Eliot Letters*, ed. Gordon S. Haight,
9 vols. (1954-78), III, 17: hereafter referred to as *Letters*.

prevailed ever since, with Henry James, for example, summarising it as "the *jeu d'esprit* of a mind that is not often — perhaps not often enough — found at play"[2]; Marghanita Laski condemning it as "a sadly poor supernatural story"[3]; and Christopher Ricks dismissing it as "the weirdest fiction she ever wrote"[4]. On the whole, though, the critical (and editorial) tendency has been tactfully to overlook its existence.

George Eliot's own initial diffidence concerning the tale would seem to prompt these attitudes. As though anticipating James' remark, she described it to John Blackwood before sending it to him as "a slight story of an outré kind — not a *jeu d'esprit*, but a *jeu de melancolie*"[5]. However, fourteen years later, her reply to Blackwood, when he wrote claiming that his admiration for the story had grown and asking permission to republish it in a new *Tales from Blackwood* series, shows that her stance had changed considerably:

> Apropos of *The Lifted Veil*, I think it will not be judicious to reprint it at present. I care for the idea

2. George Eliot's 'The Lifted Veil' and 'Brother Jacob' in *A Century of George Eliot Criticism*, ed. Gordon S. Haight (1966), p.131; the review first appeared in the *Nation*, 25th April 1878, p.277.

3. *George Eliot and her World* (1973), p.71.

4. "She was still young" BBC Radio 3, 3rd December 1980. See also Christopher Ricks, "It was her books to which she gave birth", *Listener*, 11th December 1980, p.786.

5. *Letters*, III, 41.

which it embodies and which justifies its painfulness.
A motto which I wrote on it yesterday perhaps is
sufficient indication of that idea: —

> Give me no light, great heaven, but such as turns
> To energy of human fellowship;
> No powers save the growing heritage
> That makes completer manhood.

But it will be well to put the story in harness with some
other productions of mine, and not send it forth in its
dismal loneliness. There are many things in it which
I would willingly say over again, and I shall never put
them in any other form. But we must wait a little.
The question is not in the least one of money, but of
care for the best effect of writing, which often depends
on circumstances much as pictures depend on light
and juxtaposition.[6]

With the slightly altered motto now its epigraph, *The
Lifted Veil* in fact reappeared after a lapse of another five
years, sandwiched — at the Lewes' own request — between
Silas Marner and *Brother Jacob* in the Cabinet edition of
George Eliot's works, a fate which has perhaps helped to
hide rather than to "harness" it. Nevertheless, it is clear
from her tone that the author had ceased to regard it as a
jeu of any kind: on the contrary, it embodies an idea that
was, and remained, important to her, and that she wished
the reader to have the opportunity of taking seriously.

---

6. *Letters*, V, 380.

Marghanita Laski's evaluation aside, the problem with the story seems to be less its literary quality (Henry James, at least, was able to see that it was "a fine piece of writing", and John Blackwood always conceded that it was powerful) than the apparent subject matter; for in *The Lifted Veil* George Eliot has accompanied her clairvoyant, first person narrator, Latimer, into a realm where her admirers do not expect, or wish, to find her. Even her biographer, Gordon Haight, sympathises with her publisher's difficulty in having to write to her about it. But *The Lifted Veil* is more than just an exercise in Victorian sensationalism, in spite of its use of the conventions that are more readily associated with Edgar Allan Poe or Wilkie Collins, or even (it has been suggested) with Mary E. Braddon. It is true that George Eliot's *treatment* of her idea is a departure for her, and therefore requires a corresponding adjustment on the part of the reader. Nevertheless, it is the idea itself which is important to her; and what her letter to Blackwood emphasises is that she wishes to justify the story's painfulness, not its unorthodoxy. The unbiased question that presents itself, then, is: does *The Lifted Veil* fulfil the idea that the solemn motto expresses? If we look behind Latimer's visionary excursions to the forsaken and the unknown, and behind his unenviable ability to peer into other people's petty, selfish minds, I think the answer is that it does; for his story, like that of all George Eliot's protagonists, is essentially a moral journey. Preternatural though his gifts are, his spiritual predicament is created through his misinterpretation or misapplication of what is revealed to him: his curse is not, as he thinks, his clairvoyance, but his inability to reconcile its discoveries with his immediate desire for what does not properly belong to him.

Possessing "the poet's sensibility without his voice", Latimer's greatest yearning is for inspiration, and he exults in his first vision in the mistaken belief that it could be a manifestation of "spontaneous creation". This is a perverse response, for, as though it were a reflection of his own artistic barrenness and "fatal solitude of soul", the Prague that has broken in upon his consciousness is a city devoid of hope or purpose: trapped in its own aridity and condemned to a meaningless perpetuity, it represents a form of self-perpetrated hell. Latimer is in no doubt as to the misery of the inhabitants of the visionary city, who are doomed to live on "without the repose of night or the new birth of morning". Nevertheless he sees their images neither as presages of his own destiny nor as mere figments of a perhaps fevered imagination, but as poetic fancies painted by his "newly-liberated genius". In electing to follow this false genius, he unwittingly chooses the path that is illuminated by the light of lost souls: the light that George Eliot repudiates in her motto. He does not follow passively, but earns his eventual fate by concentrating all his warped longing in efforts to bring about other such experiences, and, although he finds he cannot determine how or when they will come, his efforts are rewarded with a series of spontaneous visions that are not the Dantean journeys he had hoped for, but projections of the forms in which temptation will appear to him and revelations of the consequences of succumbing to that temptation. The first of these is, like the Prague vision, infused with warning. There is neither innocence nor kindness associated with Bertha's thin-lipped, faery, "fatal-eyed" prefiguration. She materialises "like a birth from some cold sedgy stream", a "water-nixie" whose charms, redolent of death, are reminiscent of the consumptive Keats' "Belle Dame Sans Merci."[7]

As his subsequent visions become more explicit, Latimer discovers that the intoxicating mystery — intoxicating because her mind is the *only* mystery now remaining to him — of the actual, breathing Bertha, will be transformed into murderous malevolence if she becomes his wife; but the choice either to spurn or to court what he is shown remains his. This is the central moral factor of the story. Latimer's prescience reveals only the consequences of his actions, not his predetermined fate: it is because of his wilful blindness to his foreseen lot as he abjectly binds himself to Bertha that he

---

7. Such creatures lurked in George Eliot's imagination even while she was writing *Adam Bede*. Describing the "tiny round holes" left in Hetty Sorrel's ears when their rings are taken out, the narrator says: "Perhaps water-nixies, and such lovely things without souls, have these little round holes in their ears by nature." (Ch. 22)

74

is conducted ineluctably towards spiritual isolation; and it is that most wretched of human conditions that her unusual means allow George Eliot, just once, to explore. But, having started on *The Mill on the Floss* with its loving evocation of Maggie Tulliver's childhood Eden, why should she have wanted to?

About six weeks before *The Lifted Veil* was finished, George Eliot's sister Chrissey (Christiana Evans Clarke) had died of consumption. Influenced by her once-adored brother, the author's family had disowned her since they had become aware of her illicit marriage to Lewes. But Chrissey had written from her sick-bed less than three weeks before she died a conciliatory letter that "ploughed up"[8] George Eliot's heart, and she told her old friend Sara Hennell that "Chrissey's death has taken from the possibility of many things towards which I looked with some hope and yearning in the future".[9] Chrissey's death before the promise of reunion could be fulfilled must have reactivated memories of other blighted family affections, and it seems to me that an element of her own mourning for that kinship is projected and magnified through the alienation from his fellow mortals that Latimer ultimately endures. It is not surprising that his story took brief precedence over *The Mill on the Floss*, for, although Maggie was to suffer social banishment after having been

---

8. *Letters*, III, 23.
9. Ibid, 38.

75

cast off, like her author, by her censorious brother, her story was to be one of generosity, moral struggle, and moral triumph. Her refusal to accept a happiness that is at the expense of others is rewarded with the blessing of "one supreme moment" of reconciliation-in-death with her brother Tom, which comes only when she has been reconciled one by one with all those she loves best. Latimer's criteria are the reverse of Maggie's. His persistent quest for fulfilment is no more than a quest for self-gratification, no matter what the cost to others or the future cost to himself, and it earns him the protracted torment of alienation from humanity itself which culminates in a death bereft of consolation. The very fact that his pitiable fate is the negative of Maggie's demonstrates that George Eliot's imagination had not deserted its proper path, but that it had only set out to expose the opposite destination; and by getting Latimer to tell his own story she is able, in a sense, to disclaim its spirit: not for nothing is he the "deviant" (as Barbara Hardy aptly describes him)[10] among George Eliot's otherwise affirmative narrators. But, however dismal his story is, to write it was also, perhaps, cathartic, since all that is deemed to be autobiographical in the resumed *Mill on the Floss* celebrates ties that, for all the anguish caused by social and fraternal rejection, are *un*alienable.

No one familiar with George Eliot's novels could find

---

10. *Particularities* (1982), p.143.

her preoccupation in *The Lifted Veil* with a certain kind of egoism uncharacteristic. Her moral philosophy is implicit in her shaping of Latimer's destiny. What appears to be uncharacteristic is that the undoubted power of the story is generated by "supernatural" or "weird" means. But if we take into consideration the pursuits and beliefs of the friends with whom Marian Evans spent much of her time before Lewes entered and anchored her life and gave her the confidence to become George Eliot, we can see that the material for *The Lifted Veil* was — like much of the material for *The Mill on the Floss* — drawn from her past. Her close friendship with Charles and Cara Bray — whose Coventry home, Rosehill, continued to be Marian's sanctuary after she had moved to London to become assistant editor of the *Westminster Review* — not only weaned her from evangelicalism, but encouraged her imagination to engage with the interrelated and highly topical subjects of phrenology, mesmerism (or animal magnetism), and clairvoyance. Though now largely debunked, each of these fields was then attracting its own specific investigators, fanatics, and charlatans, but George Eliot's correspondence illustrates the fact that many intelligent and educated Victorians were prepared to give one or the other — or even all three — of these phenomena their serious attention.

She became acquainted with representatives of all the categories: Harriet Martineau, for example, who thought

mesmerism "a power sacred to higher purposes";[11]
Herbert Spencer, who temporarily espoused the phrenol-
ogical cause, contributing three articles in 1844 to *The
Zoist* (which described itself as "A Journal of Cerebral
Physiology and Mesmerism and their Application to
Human Welfare"); and the founder of that journal,
Dr John Elliotson, whose mesmeric practices fascinated
his friend Charles Dickens but cost him his chair in
Medicine at the University of London. The believers
and practitioners did not always correspond in their
deductions. They urged their evidence and counter-
evidence publicly and often bitterly. With their physio-
logical approach, the phrenologists asked excited and
alarming questions as to the relationship between
inherent cerebral characteristics and moral capacity,
questions that the mesmerists enthusiastically explored.
Mesmerised subjects (or victims, as many indignant
observers saw them) in their turn often became — or
claimed to become — clairvoyant while in their induced
trance. Other clairvoyants volunteered astonishing
accounts of visions that came to them spontaneously.

Charles Bray, who was himself an ardent convert to
phrenology and its lifelong advocate, testifies in his
autobiography to Marian's interest in the subject.[12]
We know that in 1844, when she was twenty-four, she

11. *Letters on Mesmerism* (1845), p.51.
12. *Phases of Opinion and Experience during a Long Life:
An Autobiography* (1884), p.74.

submitted to having a cast made of her head for him, while her letters frequently offered brief phrenological descriptions. Bray introduced her to the utterly committed Edinburgh phrenologist George Combe, who had already been so impressed with her cast that he thought it was a man's. Combe was delighted with the intellectual power she manifested in phrenological debate. It is well known that she was later to scandalise him with her "morbid mental aberration"[13] in going off with the already-married Lewes, who was in any case contemptuous of Combe's phrenological views; but Marian had initially been almost as impressed with Combe as he had been with her, describing him to Sara Hennell as "an apostle. An apostle, it is true, with a back and front drawing-room, but still earnest, convinced, consistent, having fought a good fight."[14] Their correspondence — both professional and personal — flourished until Marian's liaison with Lewes put an end to the relationship, and it is probably from this correspondence (of which some significant items have escaped Gordon Haight's formidable edition of George Eliot's letters) that Latimer's experiences are evolved.

In March 1852, Combe wrote to Marian reporting that he had heard that the *Westminster Review* "will not admit even an incidental allusion, if respectful, to such subjects

---

13. *Letters*, VIII, 129.
14. *Letters*, II, 61.

as Mesmerism and Phrenology. It ignores them altogether as topics of human thought or Scientific investigation."[15] Marian answered that, although this was "false", the difficulty was

> that the great majority of "investigators" of mesmerism are anything but "scientific". The reason for excluding that or any other subject of moment from the Review, would be the difficulty of getting it adequately treated. An ordinary pilot will do for plain sailing, but we want clear vision and long experience when we set out on voyages of discovery.[16]

It is unlikely that she was merely being tactful. Having herself been mesmerised in July 1844 "to the degree that she could not open her eyes",[17] she certainly did not dismiss all mesmerists as charlatans. In any case, Combe was not put off, for he sent her by return of post the following newsletter, which I quote at length since it illustrates the grip that the activities of William Gregory, Edinburgh University's Professor of Chemistry, had on the public's imagination:

> In the Edinburgh newspapers a series of Letters by Professor Gregory & others on clairvoyance have lately

---

15. MS 7392, 30th March 1852; folio 543, National Library of Scotland. This extract was first published in B. M. Gray: "Pseudo-science and George Eliot's 'The Lifted Veil'" (*Nineteenth-Century Fiction*; March 1982, p.410).

16. *Letters*, VIII, 41.

17. *Letters*, I, 180.

been exciting much discussion. Dr James Coxe, a complete sceptic in this branch of mesmerism, came to me last week & begged of me to give him some piece of MS to put the powers of Professor Gregory's patient to the test. I gave him a letter dated 10 May 1838 written by the late Mr Richard Carmichael, of Dublin, containing nothing but his commentary on my translation of "Gall on the cerebellum" & an invitation to visit him. Mrs Gregory put the woman asleep. Dr Coxe & she were the only persons present besides the patient.
Dr Coxe put the letter in the latter's hands, folded so that she could not read it. Mrs Gregory did not know what the letter contained, or by whom it was written. The patient said "you must take me to some place." Dr Coxe named Dublin, & nothing more. She then told him that the writer was a handsome man, like an officer, but not one. She saw him in a study among papers. She then saw him in a long room raised at the end, & he was speaking to a number of young men. All this was literally correct, for he had a fine military air, wrote a good deal, & was lecturer to the Royal College of Surgeons, at the date of the letter. Dr Coxe asked — "Is this his present occupation?" She paused, & shuddered. "No — He is drowned. It is not a shipwreck, but I see him in the water! I see an animal with him, it is swimming like a dog, but it is too big — oh! it is a horse! there are two or three men calling him to swim:
He swims! He sinks! He is drowned! His horse is alive!"
All this was literally true. Mr Carmichael was drowned in June 1849 crossing the sands near Howth on horse-

back! & two or three men saw him, & called to him:
& his horse reached the shore. Dr Coxe told me these
results in profound amazement; and neither he nor I can
throw a ray of light upon them. He went to the patient,
because he thought that leading questions had been put
by other enquirers, & he resolved to give no other clue
to the patient or Mrs Gregory to arrive at the facts by
guessing. There must be much in this world which we
have not yet dreamt of in our philosophy.[18]

Another experiment — this time a failure — with the same
patient was also duly reported to Marian. Both accounts
interested her greatly, and in her letter of thanks for them
she told Combe that "indications of claire-voyance
witnessed by a competent observer are of thrilling interest
and give me a restless desire to get at more extensive and
satisfactory evidence."[19]

The indications are that she did "get at" such evidence;
for Latimer's experiences correspond remarkably closely
to testimonies that William Gregory had published the
previous year in *Letters to a Candid Inquirer on Animal
Magnetism*, which — as a reviewer contemptuously put
it — requires us

> to believe that there are individuals who can tell us
> what is taking place at the moment in localities which
> they have never visited, what is being done by persons

---

18. MS 7392, 10 April 1852; folios 548-54, National Library of
Scotland. This extract was first published in Gray, op. cit., p.411.
19. *Letters*, VIII, 45.

whom they never saw, what is being thought or felt by
individuals of whose personality they had no previous
knowledge; who can inform us of the entire past history
of such individuals, and can predict their future course
and destination . . . from whose mental vision, in fact,
nothing can be concealed, if only it happens to take the
required direction, which (it is admitted) cannot always
be secured.[20]

Latimer is exactly such an individual. His "wonderfully
distinct vision" of Prague — of which he had not seen
so much as a picture — and the succeeding visions of
unknown cities and foreign landscapes, are reminiscent
of the visions of Professor Gregory's patient Mr "D", a
medical student who, it was claimed, became clairvoyant
when in a deep mesmeric sleep, and described places he
had never visited and people he had never met. According
to Professor Gregory, Mr "D" saw Cologne, for example,

in a bird's-eye view, or as from a balloon, in which way
I certainly never saw it, nor thought of it. He noticed
the river, the bridge of boats, many spires, and one very
large building, much higher than the rest. I begged him
to [approach] nearer to it, and he soon spoke of being
in a street, where his attention was arrested by a fat,
jolly-looking old boy, as he called him, standing in the
doorway of his shop, without a hat, and with an apron
on. At my request, he described the exterior of the large

20. *Quarterly Review*, 93 (1853), 537.

building, at one part, where he spoke of very tall
windows, the shape of which he drew, and of buttresses
and pinnacles between them. As he was much struck
with the size of the building, I conclude it was the
Dom, and that he first saw the outside of the choir, and
eastward part.[21]

Mr "D" also gives a perfect description of Bonn. Further-
more, when given a special crystal to hold, he follows a
dark-complexioned foreigner on a visionary journey
through unknown territories that include eastern Europe,
ancient Greece, and South Africa. Although these visions
cannot be verified, the mere fact that he is able, "in a
certain state, to see and describe accurately towns, such as
Aix and Cologne, countries, and persons, at a great
distance, and quite unknown to him," [22] disposes Gregory
to believe that the other visions are of real places.

Professor Gregory was equally convinced of the existence of "sympathetic clairvoyance" — the ability to read
the thoughts of others, which for George Eliot's Latimer
is a cursed affliction; and his belief "that clairvoyants do
possess the power of seeing contemporary or present
events, as well as that of seeing past events",[23] leads him
to suggest:"If past occurrences leave a trace behind them,

---

21. William Gregory, *Letters to a Candid Inquirer on Animal
Magnetism* (1851), p.427.
22. Ibid, p.439.
23. Ibid, p.158.

may not coming events cast a shadow before?"[24] Sufferers
of certain kinds of disease, for example

> will often, quite spontaneously, predict the precise time
> of one or more attacks; they will describe their intensity,
> and specify their duration; and frequently do so long
> before their occurrence, so that the necessary precautions
> may be taken.
>
> They further announce, and not unfrequently, especially
> when under magnetic treatment, that the first, second,
> third, or other attack, to take place on a certain day,
> at an hour and minute named, will be the last. And all
> these predictions are very frequently fulfilled, quite
> independently of any regularity, nay, along with the
> utmost irregularity, in the recurrence of the attacks.[25]

No necessary precautions are taken to prevent Latimer's
heart attack from being fatal. It is integral to his vision
(and to his method of narration) that it should *be* fatal.
But his experiences would surely have been celebrated by
Gregory (who died one year before *The Lifted Veil* was
finished) as a triumph of spontaneous prevision.

The important difference between *The Lifted Veil* and
Professor Gregory's case histories is in the use to which

---

24. Ibid, p.159. Gregory is quoting — or misquoting — Thomas
Campbell's second-sighted Wizard in "Lochiel's Warning" (1801):

> 'Tis the sunset of life gives me mystical lore,
> And coming events cast their shadows before.

25. Ibid, p.164.

the material is put: George Eliot is concerned with making moral fiction; Gregory with presenting evidence. What is striking, however, is George Eliot's adherence in her tale to the "facts" as Gregory describes and interprets them. She treats his beliefs and speculations with enough imaginative respect to explore their implications, even if we must infer that the veil is better left unlifted. She rejects the idea that visionary travels, like those of Gregory's patients, manifest the marvellous powers of the human mind, presenting Latimer's revelations instead as refractions of her own vision of hell as a hideously illuminated spiritual wasteland. It is a hell that Latimer eventually fully inhabits because, in the manner of Faust, he accepts what "is only to take effect at a distant day" as the price to be paid for the gratification of his immediate desires. He fails to heed Gregory's shadows cast by coming events, which to Latimer

> were only like presentiments intensified to horror. You
> have known the powerlessness of ideas before the might
> of impulse; and my visions, when once they had passed
> into memory, were mere ideas — pale shadows that
> beckoned in vain, while my hand was grasped by the
> living and the loved.

But the fleeting delights of the present are no recompense for the sacrifice of the future. Since his clairvoyance is not omniscience, but a travesty of omniscience, nothing is revealed to him that is divinely inspired, — he finds none of the Divine Pity that Maggie appeals to in the *Mill*. He is given no light but the pitiless light that was shed in his first vision; he gains no wisdom except the knowledge — George Eliot's knowledge — that

> there is no short cut, no patent tram-road, to wisdom: after all the centuries of invention, the soul's path lies through the thorny wilderness which must still be trodden in solitude, with bleeding feet, with sobs for help, as it was trodden by them of old time.

Even the revivification of the expired servant who had had a sinister power over Bertha is staged only to intensify the cruel visionary light that at first Latimer had welcomed. On the surface, the transfusion of Dr Meunier's own blood straight into the neck vein of the corpse does seem preposterously melodramatic, but it is described quite perfunctorily. The narrative drives on towards the climax, which is not the momentary success of the operation, but the shock of the posthumous release of Mrs Archer's malice. That malice is the force which brings her back from the dead; Dr Meunier's "scientific" expertise merely provides the machinery in an experiment that advances knowledge only of the futility that Latimer's existence already exemplifies. This is important, because *The Lifted Veil* is to be distinguished from contemporary supernatural sensationalism of the kind represented by Poe's "The Facts in the Case of M. Valdemar" (with which George Eliot's story has a superficial affinity) in that the *frisson* is not the main objective. The experiment on Poe's M. Valdemar — who is mesmerised "*in articulo mortis*", with the result that he is preserved in a kind of limbo for seven months — depends for its effectiveness on its presentation as a spectacularly horrifying case history recounted by the mesmerist (the story's Professor Gregory, as it were). When M. Valdemar's soul is finally allowed to depart from his body, we are meant to experience a delicious paroxysm of disgust at the proffered spectacle of a "nearly liquid mass of loathsome — of detestable putridity" that lies in the place of the undead body.

George Eliot's own use of supernatural elements and pseudo-scientific inquiry undeniably makes *The Lifted Veil* a horror story born of its time. It is the serious end to which she puts these elements that makes it also properly representative of her work. But if she uses the powers that Gregory and others were so excitedly "proving" and celebrating only in order to create a metaphorical landscape over which Latimer is doomed spiritually to wander, they were powers in which she had herself shown keen interest. Of course, the story cannot be construed as evidence that she was persuaded by Gregory's type of evidence, but it does not disown her interest; and while it is true that, as a topic, clairvoyance belonged to her pre-Lewes days, the state of trance that was its concomitant is presented, in varying forms, frequently in her fiction. Caterina Sarti in "Mr Gilfil's Love-Story" (which preceded *The Lifted Veil*) lies staring and virtually catatonic after discovering Captain Wybrow's corpse (Mr Gilfil imagines her "with the dry scorching stare of insanity"); Maggie Tulliver is in a memoryless trance of bliss and freedom from responsibility as she is "borne along by the tide" with Stephen Guest; and Silas Marner's catalepsy is the condition on which both his effect on others, and the plot, depend. On the one hand, it is a socially-isolating, awesome affliction like temporary death (Mr Macy, the parish clerk, has the splendid idea in the first chapter of *Silas Marner* that "there might be such a thing as a man's soul being loose from his body, and going out and in, like a bird out of its nest and back" — an instance, perhaps, of George Eliot's mind *really* at play); and, on the other hand, it becomes a benign power with an "invisible wand" that arrests Silas in the midst of his despair so that Eppie — whose mother has coincidentally passed through an opium trance into death — can toddle redeemingly into his life.

The conclusions of George Eliot's imaginative speculations concerning visionary trances are melancholy without being in the least trivialising. Indeed, to trivialise her material would have been to trivialise her characteristic moral — that the heedless pursuit of selfish gratification is death to the soul. Her real theme, though, is not clairvoyance, but the horror — her own horror — of alienation; and the ability to express this horror in a gripping, first-person narrative is a tribute to her inventiveness, not to her weirdness. But though the fact that she wrote it immediately after the death of an estranged sister gives a certain perspective to the impulse behind the fiction, it is worth noting that she drew for her material on her recent, happy experiences with the man with whom she lived so comfortably, as well as on her Coventry past. Latimer's journey to Prague — where his nightmarish prescience is confirmed — follows exactly the journey that she and Lewes had made companionably the year before. Even Latimer's response in Vienna to the death-exuding portrait of Lucrezia Borgia — which afterwards transforms itself into a suffocatingly malignant prevision of his future wife — is drawn from her own response, for the picture "with the cruel, cruel eyes" (as she described it in her journal)[26] was, of the many that she saw at the Belvedere, one of the few to lodge in her memory.

It is fitting, then, to allow the final comment on the story to come from Lewes, who was its first admirer, and whose unpretentious enthusiasm places *The Lifted Veil* in its proper perspectives of period and *genre*. "You must prepare for a surprise with the new story G. E. is writing," he wrote unavailingly to John Blackwood. "It is *totally* unlike anything he has written yet. The novel

---

26. See *George Eliot's Life as related in her Letters and Journals*, ed. J. W. Cross, Vols. 11-13 of *The Works of George Eliot*, Cabinet ed. (1878-85)

[i.e. *The Mill on the Floss*] will be a companion picture to Adam Bede; but this story is of an imaginative philosophical kind, quite new and piquant."[27]

Beryl Gray, London, 1984

---

27. *Letters*, III, 55.

FOR THE BEST IN PAPERBACKS, LOOK FOR THE

In every corner of the world, on every subject under the sun, Penguin represents quality and variety—the very best in publishing today.

For complete information about books available from Penguin—including Puffins, Penguin Classics, and Arkana—and how to order them, write to us at the appropriate address below. Please note that for copyright reasons the selection of books varies from country to country.

In the United Kingdom: Please write to *Dept. JC, Penguin Books Ltd, FREEPOST, West Drayton, Middlesex UB7 0BR.*

If you have any difficulty in obtaining a title, please send your order with the correct money, plus ten percent for postage and packaging, to *P.O. Box No. 11, West Drayton, Middlesex UB7 0BR*

In the United States: Please write to *Consumer Sales, Penguin USA, P.O. Box 999, Dept. 17109, Bergenfield, New Jersey 07621-0120.* VISA and MasterCard holders call 1-800-253-6476 to order all Penguin titles

In Canada: Please write to *Penguin Books Canada Ltd, 10 Alcorn Avenue, Suite 300, Toronto, Ontario M4V 3B2*

In Australia: Please write to *Penguin Books Australia Ltd, P.O. Box 257, Ringwood, Victoria 3134*

In New Zealand: Please write to *Penguin Books (NZ) Ltd, Private Bag 102902, North Shore Mail Centre, Auckland 10*

In India: Please write to *Penguin Books India Pvt Ltd, 706 Eros Apartments, 56 Nehru Place, New Delhi 110 019*

In the Netherlands: Please write to *Penguin Books Netherlands bv, Postbus 3507, NL-1001 AH Amsterdam*

In Germany: Please write to *Penguin Books Deutschland GmbH, Metzlerstrasse 26, 60594 Frankfurt am Main*

In Spain: Please write to *Penguin Books S. A., Bravo Murillo 19, 1° B, 28015 Madrid*

In Italy: Please write to *Penguin Italia s.r.l., Via Felice Casati 20, I-20124 Milano*

In France: Please write to *Penguin France S. A., 17 rue Lejeune, F–31000 Toulouse*

In Japan: Please write to *Penguin Books Japan, Ishikiribashi Building, 2–5–4, Suido, Bunkyo-ku, Tokyo 112*

In Greece: Please write to *Penguin Hellas Ltd, Dimocritou 3, GR–106 71 Athens*

In South Africa: Please write to *Longman Penguin Southern Africa (Pty) Ltd, Private Bag X08, Bertsham 2013*